SELKIE

ff

SELKIE

Kenneth Lillington

faber and faber
LONDON · BOSTON

First published in 1985
by Faber and Faber Limited
3 Queen Square London WC1N 3AU

Printed in Great Britain by
Butler & Tanner Ltd, Frome and London

© Kenneth Lillington, 1985

British Library Cataloguing in Publication Data

Lillington, Kenneth
Selkie.
I. Title
823'.914 [F]   PR6062.14
ISBN 0–571–13421–1

For
Catherine Lynch

NINETEEN THIRTY-FIVE

1

The house agent's blurb described the house as "in need of modernization". In fact, it was practically in need of rebuilding.

It stood alone on the height of the cliff, well away from the cluster of fishermen's cottages down below. The walls were of stone, and strong enough, and surprisingly, all the windows were unbroken, but inside almost everything needed renewing. It had last been occupied in 1905, thirty years before, and then, it seemed, not for long. It was lighted downstairs by gas. Upstairs there was no lighting at all. Remains of paint blotched the woodwork like a disease. The kitchen floor was so pitted that there was danger of twisting your ankle. The kitchen sink was at a height about three inches above the average knee. It was also shallow, and splashed you when you turned the tap on. This was the only tap in the house. There was no bathroom, nor was there an inside lavatory, only a squat stone structure at the end of the garden—or rather, what had once been the garden; its fences were now down, so that from the back door an unbounded riot of long grass, yellow gorse and purple heather reached to the edge of the cliff.

Wrinkling her nose, Cathy picked her way among the gorse to this outhouse. There was a soft, sticky ripping of cobwebs as she opened the door. So much rust had fallen from the cistern and its chain that the rickety wooden seat was sanded all over with it. She pictured hordes of obscene vermin, not meant for the light of day, lurking in the corners. Shuddering, she imagined using this place at night. It was just as well that her mother had brought a supply of chamberpots.

She went back to where her parents stood, displaced and numb, among their smart modern furniture and collection of silver.

"Well, we got it for a song," said her father.

"You should have given them a dirge," said Cathy.

"Never mind, there's a general handyman chap from Marazion coming to clean it all up. It's funny," said her father, "but I expected his estimate to be waiting for me when I arrived. I wonder if there's a delay in the post? I directed several other letters on, too. Should be here by now."

But none had come, and after making a round of the village, Mrs Gascoyne came back with disturbing news.

"The tradespeople won't deliver," she said. "They refuse to call on the house. That's the milkman, the baker and the greengrocer. They all made the most absurd excuses."

"Perhaps it's because we're 'foreigners'," said Mr Gascoyne. "Village folk can be very clannish."

"Oh, no, Cornish folk are very friendly as a rule, and used to visitors," said his wife. "It's this house."

"What do you mean?"

"I don't know," said Mrs Gascoyne, sinking on to a steel-tube chair. "Perhaps it's haunted. That's all we need!"

"Oh! It probably is," said Mr Gascoyne lightly, too lightly. "According to the locals, that is. We're in a different country, you know. It's not like the rest of

England. They're tremendously superstitious here. They live in a world of warlocks and pixies and mystic spells. The shops are full of magic charms."

"And are run by people with Yorkshire accents," said Cathy.

"Oh well," sighed her mother, "so long as they keep it all to themselves."

"Oh, I don't know," said Mr Gascoyne, still too lightly. "I'd love to see a warlock, so long as he'd stay still long enough for me to draw him. Mystical pictures can sell for a lot of money."

Pretending to be happy here was going to be a strain.

Until a few months ago, Cathy's father had been an artist in a London advertising agency, earning a handsome income of five hundred and fifty pounds a year. Then the agency merged with a bigger one, and he found himself out of a job. The stark truth was that the newcomers demanded new styles of commercial art which he, at forty-eight, was too old to learn.

When he came home with the news, shattered, his wife ceased to be the nagging creature he was resigned to living with, and rallied superbly to his support.

"Well," she said, "you've always wanted to be a proper painter. Now's your chance."

"I haven't a hope in hell."

"Yes you have. We'll sell this house and buy one somewhere in Cornwall. We should do well out of that, so we won't have to starve for a while. We'll sell the car, too. And quite soon you'll be selling your pictures. We'll be all right. You'll see."

She was a tower of strength.

Good for her.

But what Cathy could not stomach was all the bluff that went with it.

3

"Of course, we've been meaning to do this for *years*," Mrs Gascoyne assured her neighbours. "I've always known he was not *fulfilling* himself at that agency."

Not that the needle-eyed neighbours were deceived for a minute, nor were they displeased, for they had always envied the Gascoynes. But they pretended to admire him. How brave of him to burn his boats!

And what about Cathy, the light of the Sixth Form?

"Well, you know, she's really *outgrown* that school," confided Mrs Gascoyne. "She'll go to a good school in Cornwall if she wishes, but between ourselves, I think she's longing to get out into the world."

It wasn't true. Cathy was no happier at school than anyone normally is, but all her friends were there, and she hated leaving it. As for "getting out into the world", this meant, probably, going to a commercial school in Truro to learn shorthand-typing. She would just as soon have faced a stretch in Holloway.

Then there was Clive. He was the son of one of Mrs Gascoyne's friends. Cathy was, she supposed, his girl-friend. She didn't know for certain. Clive was fair-haired, long-limbed, and clean-cut enough to be on the cover of a boy's annual. He had already achieved greatness, being the captain of his public school, and also captain of games. The school was situated nearby, and Clive came home at weekends, and usually honoured Cathy with a visit. He apologized for her to his friends, because he was self-conscious about having a girl-friend. "Actually," he told them deprecatingly, "I like having her around because she's a jolly good tennis player." They were secretly awed. "Preston-Browne's got a woman," they told one another.

Cathy was not quite so impressed by his status as she ought to have been, but when the time came to move she felt a sudden new longing for him.

"I'm having to leave everybody and everything," she told him piteously.

"Oh, rotten luck," he said.

He stood looking at her uncertainly.

"When do you leave?" he asked eventually.

"Tomorrow morning. Will you come and see me off?"

"Tomorrow *mor*-ning . . . Saturday . . . It's rather awkward, actually . . . You see, there's Nets . . ."

"Couldn't you give them a miss for once?"

"Well . . . You see, one can't really cut Nets . . ."

"So we won't see each other again."

Once more the uncertain, well-bred gaze.

"Will you miss me, Clive?"

"Yes, rather."

Cathy went out later that day and found a rambling, crumbling path that led to the beach. The tiny village they had come to, Polraddon, was not the haunt of tourists, and the strip of beach below their bit of cliff was, the house agent had exultantly pointed out, "secluded". Yes, extremely secluded. A positive desert. Even the fishermen avoided it.

The sea looked lovely, a rippling carpet of liquid brilliance in the afternoon sun. Yet even that was unfriendly. She had been severely warned against swimming here. There were treacherous currents.

She sat on a rock at the edge of the water and gazed dejectedly out. She started. A dark head moved across her view some twenty yards out to sea. So swift and streamlined was the swimmer that she thought at first it might be a seal; there were seals on this coast. But in fact it was a girl, with long hair streaming free.

Cathy loved swimming. With more practice she might have made county standard, but her school discouraged specialization. However, neither she nor even the team who were going to the Olympics in Berlin next year would have any chance against this girl. She was using a stroke Cathy had never seen before, feet together and moving like a tail, together with an overarm swing that lifted her clear to her waist. It propelled her along in a series of long, smooth leaps, as if she were a dolphin, or a seal. It was amazingly fast.

She somersaulted in the water and moved nearer to the shore. She dived under. Cathy stood up to watch her as she entered a lime-green patch of the multi-hued sea. She had her arms to her sides and was not using her limbs now, but sliding along under water like a snake, by means of sinuous writhings of her body. She remained submerged for an alarmingly long time. She broke surface, shook her head, and dived again.

She had spotted Cathy for sure, and was showing off, but such masterly showing off was it that Cathy could only gasp with admiration. Twice she gathered breath to shout, "Jolly good! Wish I could swim like you!" but twice the girl dived under, and the second time she stayed down so long that Cathy grew concerned, lest she had paid for her display by crashing her head on a rock. But then she emerged, mere feet away, standing in water up to her knees. She was brown like a bronze statue, and quite naked.

This was awkward. Cathy realized that she might be standing on the very rock where the girl had left her clothes. She had been taught, however, that it was bad manners ever to seem ill at ease, so she waved, and called pleasantly in her cut-glass voice. "Sorry! I was just taking a stroll! Didn't know you were there! Can I find your towel for you?"

The girl moved back till the water came up to her neck. She stared at Cathy with great, liquid eyes that betrayed no feeling at all. Then she turned with a swish, raced out to sea, and once again disappeared in a dive.

What was the matter with everyone here? It was certainly not a friendly place.

Still, no doubt it was too much to expect the girl to wade out as she was. One should clear off and save her further embarrassment.

Cathy trudged back as fast as the silver sand would let her, not looking round until she had reached the cliff path. There was still no sign of the girl.

A little later, Cathy went to the post office in the village to see if there was any mail for them. There was quite a bundle of it, including one envelope marked Marazion.

"Would you mind most awfully asking the postman to bring them to the house?"

"I'm afraid he won't do that, moy lover."

"Why ever not?"

"Perhaps your house is too high up the hill for his old bones."

"Have all the tradespeople round here got old bones? Because none of them will come up to our house. What's wrong with it?"

The postmistress kept smiling. She had a fixed smile on a biscuit-coloured, healthy face, with cornflower-blue eyes.

"Do tell me," said Cathy.

"We-ell . . . The folk of Polraddon are very superstitious. I'm from Devon myself, but I've been here thirty years, and I know them. They're friendly folk, but they won't go near your house or your stretch of beach."

"Why not?"

"Ah, now. They just won't."

"Well, there's one who will, anyway."

"Oh? Who's that?"

"There was a girl swimming off our beach this

7

afternoon."

The smile faded.

"What was she like?"

Cathy hesitated. The postmistress lowered her voice.

"Was she naked?"

Cathy coloured a little. The word "naked" was thought rather indelicate in her society.

"Oh, yes, absolutely in the altogether. I suppose she thought she had the place to herself."

"A good swimmer? Very very good?"

"Yes, marvellous."

"Don't tell anyone about this. And I should stay away from that beach, if I were you."

They went upstairs carrying candles, just as the very first occupants must have done, over a hundred years ago. Cathy stood on the small bedside rug, an island in the bare wooden planks, and undressed gingerly. She tiptoed distastefully over to her wardrobe, hung up her clothes, and thought of all the mice who had probably gathered, in long generations of beady eyes, behind the skirting boards. She went to pin up Clark Gable, cut out of *Picturegoer*, over her bed, but couldn't bear to see him degraded by the filthy distempered wall. She got into bed in her yellow pyjamas, blew out the candle, and gave herself up to yearning for the home she had left. Oh! to sleep in her old bedroom, for all its smallness, to rejoin her friends, for all their limitations, to play tennis again with Clive, for all his conceit!

But she couldn't even be nostalgic in peace. This place was never free from the sound of the seagulls. They wheeled incessantly over the cliffs, uttering their derisive, lamenting cries, and at intervals they all settled on the roof of the house, a thousand or a million of them, and rent and shattered the air. They seemed so close to her very bed that Cathy was alarmed against her reason, as one can be by thunder.

Then they all suddenly rose and flew off into the distance, their screeching dying away over the sea. A new sound made itself heard.

It was a woman singing, it came from the direction of the cliffs, and it was drawing nearer the house.

Cathy's room was at the back of the house, overlooking the cliff. She went to the window, but it was almost opaque. Nor could she open it; she had tried this once before, and it had crashed back from a broken sashcord like a guillotine. She heard the sound more clearly now. It was lilting and melancholy and lonely, and it pained her to listen, as it might to hear the crying of a lost child, but it was eerie too, and she took to her bed again, and pulled the clothes over her head.

After a few seconds she emerged from cover. The singing had stopped. There was a new sound, a timid knocking at the back door.

She sat up. It sounded again, *tap*-ta-tap, *tap*-ta-tap. She got out of bed and pulled on a dressing-gown.

A glint of light passed along under her door. Her father had heard it too, and was on his way downstairs with a candle. She found a pocket torch and slipped out of her room. Her mother stood framed in the doorway of her own bedroom, scared and indignant. She croaked some sort of warning. Cathy ignored it, and joined her father on the stairs.

"So you heard it too, did you? It's probably nothing. One of the tradesmen thinking better of it, ha ha."

"Dad, it's ten past twelve."

"Perfectly simple explanation, I expect."

He put his arm round her. Cathy never liked her father to touch her, but she knew he was scared, and did not resist. They went into the kitchen and he lit the gas from his candle, making no attempt to be quiet, but, on the contrary, banging about rather unnecessarily, and talking in a near shout.

"Something perfectly normal!"

"Did you hear the singing, Dad?"

"Singing?" he barked. "What singing? I didn't hear any singing."

"There was someone singing."

"Don't get let's;" He checked himself–he really was terribly agitated. "Don't *let's get* silly fancies," he corrected himself. Cathy extricated herself discreetly from his nervous clutch.

"I suggest we open the door."

"Yes, right . . . the damn bolt is stiff," he said, panting.

It was not, but he was pushing it instead of pulling it back. Cathy released it quite easily. He shouldered her aside, took a breath, and flung the door open with a crash.

There was nothing there. He took her torch and shone it about.

"Oh! Here you are! Here's your knocking!"

He drew her outside and pulled the back door to. An ancient lantern hung from a nail just above it, and, to be sure, it did roll a little with the wind and scrape against the door.

"*Voilà!*"

But of course there was no "*voilà*" about it. It was just an excuse; the rattling of this lantern was nothing like the firm, spaced tapping they had heard.

"But–" began Cathy, but stopped. She would not challenge him; he was so anxious for reassurance.

He went back into the house. "It's all right, dear," he called. "It was an old lantern, that's all."

"An old what?"

"Lantern."

"What lantern?"

"Oh, for God's sake!" He began to climb the stairs.

"Catherine," called her mother, with dignity, "come in before you catch your death of cold."

Mr Gascoyne had hooked the lantern up on its chain so that it couldn't rattle any more, but Cathy wasn't taken in for a moment. Nor was he.

She lay in bed thinking it over.

What a long day it had been. What a strange day.

"This house *is* haunted," she told herself.

2

In daylight, however, she changed her mind. The explanation might not be as simple as her father wished it to be, but surely there was one. Cathy hated mysteries. Most of them arose, she suspected, because people preferred them to finding out the truth.

The mystery of Polraddon seemed connected with that girl who swam in the sea. She was no ghost.

And another thing: the sea in that region couldn't be as dangerous as it was said to be, because the girl had been so much at ease there. A wonderful swimmer, yes. But Cathy could take care of herself in the water, too.

The sea looked very inviting . . .

That afternoon, when both her parents were out, she put on the two-piece bathing costume of which her mother disapproved, dressed again, and went down to the beach. It was deserted as usual. The sea was calm and smooth and many-coloured, grey and green and silver and dark blue, in long bands, like roads seen from the air. She hid her clothes behind a rock and put on her bathing cap.

"Rocks," she warned herself. "Paddle carefully and get well out."

But the tide was out and all the dangerous rocks were showing, and the water was bland and delicious. It crept up to her waist and then, at a step, she was out of her depth. Gliding rather than swimming, she went out twenty-five yards. It was smooth and easy; too easy in fact, but she was a baths swimmer and knew little of the wiles of the sea. She had only to steer herself, keeping her feet together and planing with her arms. It was like freewheeling downhill. She felt triumphant. Those treacherous currents were an old wives' tale. And then the water began resisting her. It was as if she had reached the bottom of the hill and started upwards. She resorted to her strongest stroke, the breast-stroke, but she couldn't manage the usual glide with it. When she straightened out, the water heaved up and pressed her backward. There was a swell not to be seen from the shore. The water lifted and fell away, so that sometimes she kicked air. She did not seem to be advancing at all. She began fighting now, flailing so that her muscles burned. She became rather panicky. She made a sprawling turn and tried to swim back to the beach. It was like trying to push down a wall. She gulped air, put her head down, and tried to crash through in a flurried crawl. The crawl is less stabilizing than the breast-stroke. The waves picked up her streamlined body and rolled it over. She no longer knew which way she was heading. She was deep under water, holding her breath to suffocation. She slammed her arms down to her sides and felt herself rise, and she did break surface, and managed to breathe out explosively and gasp in some more air, and then the water heaved again and tipped her head over heels.

She tried to tread water. The current turned into a coil and made a corkscrew of her, slinging and twirling her legs and flinging her arms awry. A small, lazy wave rose up above her eyebrows and slapped into her mouth as she gasped, so that she swallowed water "the wrong way", and was seized with a spasm like

13

whooping cough. She was on her back with the sun in her eyes, and flung about like a jointed doll.

A Channel swimmer, meeting the flood-tide as he nears home, must sometimes swim parallel to the shore for several miles before he can land. Such a plan occurred to Cathy. Farther along the coast, swimming was safer. She must get away from this fiendish bay and somehow get ashore farther down. To walk back barefoot in her two-piece costume was not inviting, but it was better than drowning. The cliffs, tantalizingly near but unreachable, bobbed before her eyes for an instant and gave her direction. She rolled over and once again tried to swim.

She was weakened, but she made some headway. The water was easier. She could slow right down now, relax, and swim slowly and steadily for hours if necessary. Suddenly, she swam into an ice-cold patch. The toes in her left foot locked, and the cramp rose up and twisted her calf muscles in a hard knot. She trod water, beating with her arms like wings. Her leg hurt abominably. She was extremely frightened.

A dark and streaming head showed itself in the water a dozen feet away.

"Help," called Cathy in a cracked voice. *"Please."*

The head drew nearer. It was not that of the swimming girl, as she had hoped, but the head of a seal, with drooping moustaches and malevolent, inquisitive eyes. Bulky, bull-heavy, the animal nosed into Cathy's very face, and then circled her, the brutal beat of its tail rolling a wave over her head. It exuded power as she did weakness. She was at its mercy. It snorted. It turned its nose to the sky and honked, harsh and earsplitting. It barked several times. There was a disturbance in the water a little way behind it, a flash of arms, and the face of the swimming girl rose up. It was

14

grave and mild. It watched Cathy. The seal, like a sentry relieved, dived under and disappeared.

"*Help*," croaked Cathy. "*Help, please.*"

The girl stayed still, watchful like a placid cat. Her huge dark eyes were just like the seal's, but mild, even tender, but for all that she did not stir to Cathy's aid.

"Oh, *do help me.*"

The girl circled Cathy slowly, as the seal had done. Oh, God, this witless suspicion! Or was she baiting Cathy, enjoying it? What *was* this creature?

In pain, terrified, Cathy did not dare to scream for fear of driving her off. Instead she broke down and sobbed, turning and turning about in the water, flapping with her arms like a wounded bird.

The girl submerged. She rose again under Cathy, took her by the arms, thrust her clear of the water, and, still submerged, began propelling her towards the shore. She swam with terrific speed and power, riding the water, insinuating her body into its wicked currents and compelling them to her own advantage. Cathy dragged her left knee under her chin and kneaded her cramped leg as they went. From her straightened right leg she saw a long V streaming away like the wake of a steamer. In less than a minute the girl deposited her on the beach by the rock. Cathy, too knocked up for thanks, knelt there coughing and panting.

From some unseen crevice the girl produced an extraordinary garment: an enormous cloak, apparently made of seaweed. She wrapped it round Cathy; it drew the sun like a cloche, and in a few moments she became dry and warm. Cathy sat up, almost the prefect-elect again, almost Catherine.

"Thank you," she said. "Very much."

The girl, who all this time had watched Cathy's face with the closest attention, nodded and smiled. Then

15

she spoke, saying the same thing several times in a strange-sounding language. At last Cathy realized, with wonder, that it was English.

The girl said, "You live in the house," and pointed towards the cliff. She pronounced "house", "hey-yoose", in an accent burred and full of diphthongs, like some primordial ancestor of Cornish speech, but with some other tone, a foreign one, mixed into it.

"Yes, we've just moved in. We arrived yesterday."

But the girl could understand Cathy no better than Cathy could her.

"Yes. We–live–in–the–house."

The girl smiled again, and Cathy, feeling that further conversation would be too difficult, smiled back, and began to dress herself under cover of the cloak. The girl watched her with affectionate amusement, as one might watch the ritual of a pet animal. Cathy handed her the cloak, which she draped carelessly over her shoulders.

"Aren't you going to get dressed?"

No response.

"Clothes?" said Cathy, pointing to some places on her person, and flapping her skirt. "Clothes?"

The girl laughed and shook her head.

What now? Cathy owed her life to this girl, but what could be done about it? To offer her money would be not only insulting but useless, and she could not see what progress they could make socially. She held out her hand. The girl took it carefully, as though afraid of breaking something fragile.

"I'm very very grateful to you," said Cathy effusively. "You saved my life, you know. I really am most awfully . . ."

No use.

"Thank you," said Cathy. "Thank you very much. Thank you."

The girl said, "I go to the house?"

"I beg pardon?" said Cathy, with a pang of dismay. "What? What did you say?"

"I go with you to the house?"

Since birth, Cathy had been given such advice as "you should keep yourself to yourself", "it's unwise to get too familiar", and "it's best not to get involved". She despised it in her head, but it was in her blood, and hard to unlearn. So her first reaction was alarm. What would her parents say? And what–dread of their kind!–what would the neighbours say?

"Er . . ." said Cathy. She swallowed. "Er, well, that isn't awfully convenient just at present, actually . . . Look, couldn't we arrange to meet somewhere? . . ."

No, of course, the girl understood not a word of this. Cathy shook her head. "No," she said, helplessly. "No."

The girl's face fell, and Cathy saw her, as it were, for the first time, and she realized how beautiful she was. The beauties she knew were Hollywood film stars, glamorized out of all reality. This girl's beauty was from nature alone. Cathy felt small and petty and mean. It was like rejecting an angel.

"Look, I'm sorry," she babbled. "We can arrange . . . We'll meet again . . . I'll bring you some of my clothes . . ."

But the girl, though she might not understand the words, understood the tone and the attitude. She turned away, whipped off and concealed the seaweed cloak so quickly that it was like sleight of hand, and ran into the water, leaving Cathy standing there sick at heart with self-disgust, watching as she zoomed out to sea, a human torpedo, until, some fifty yards clear, she dived under.

Human?

"She's not human," said Cathy to herself. "She lives out there."

3

The handyman from Marazion turned up the next morning. His name was Stoneham. He was very young, about twenty, and very tall and spare, and goodlooking in a rugged, cheerful way. He spoke with a trace of Cockney.

Cathy's parents both addressed him in the special tones they used for the working classes, her mother condescendingly gracious, her father slangy and jokey. He towered over them, inclining his head respectfully, replying briefly and sensibly to her father's fussy questions. Cathy didn't think her parents were showing up very well, and she was a little anxious about the figure she herself was cutting.

She followed him as he inspected her own room.

"A terrible mess, isn't it?"

"Certainly a lot to be done, miss."

"You can imagine how we felt, coming here from civilization," said Cathy. "Good job we've got a sense of humour."

She followed this up with a little laugh, which immediately echoed in her ears as something completely insane. Tee-hee-hee! How idiotic! She stood there, feeling inadequate and superfluous.

"You'll practically have to pull the place down, won't you?" she said humbly, after a pause.

He smiled and nodded.

"Lots of creepy-crawlies behind there," she ventured.

"'Creepy-crawlies'," repeated the young man. (Yes, here again: what a coy, nursery affectation! What was the matter with her?) "You mean, like spiders and that?"

"Yes. Get rid of them, won't you? I hate spiders."

"Oh, yes, sure. Can't help feeling sorry for them though, can you?" added the extraordinary young man. "Being driven out of their own homes."

He looked up at Cathy's astonished face and grinned.

"You reckon that's going a bit too far, do you?"

"Well, I must say—"

"Yes, sure. Don't worry. I'll get rid of the spiders."

He gave a sort of final nod, and Cathy felt herself dismissed.

He came to terms with Mr Gascoyne and set off immediately in his van to collect some materials.

"He's cheap enough, I must say," said Mr Gascoyne. "I expected it to be more than this."

"I expect he's doing well enough out of it," said his wife.

"Oh, no doubt. Something of a rough diamond, isn't he?"

"M'm," said Mrs Gascoyne. "I rather wish we'd got a proper firm in to do this, in spite of the cost. I don't like the idea of his moving about so freely among all our things. I mean, we don't know anything about him, do we?"

"He was highly recommended to me."

"Well, we must keep an eye on him."

"Perhaps we ought to keep him on a chain," said Cathy.

"No one's condemning him, Cath," said her father pacifically. "Your mother just believes in being careful,

19

that's all."

Mrs Gascoyne was irritated. Cathy often irritated her.

"Don't get too familiar with that young man, Catherine," she said sharply. "You were talking to him much too freely, I thought. He's just a handyman, a labourer. You should not hobnob with him."

"It's a relief to hobnob with anyone down here."

"Yes, I know," said her mother, softening. "I know you're lonely. Well, as soon as we can, we'll join the church–there's a lovely old church at Pendeen, which isn't so far from here, and all the visitors go there. Well, apart from the trippers, of course. I believe it attracts a very good class of people. You'll soon make plenty of friends. I've already written to the Vicar, and I'm going to call on him as soon as I can."

"Don't tell him that Dad's out of work. It might embarrass him."

"Catherine! That remark was quite uncalled for!"

The next day Mrs Gascoyne had a problem. Her husband, wishing he had not parted with the Hillman so soon, had trudged off to try to sell his pictures to the art shops, and she herself had some shopping to do in Truro which would keep her away all day. This meant either taking Cathy with her, and leaving their valuables within the reach of a strange man, or leaving Cathy alone with him, and also, as it were, within his reach.

She decided in favour of protecting their property, warned Cathy to keep an eye on him but not to hobnob with him, and went out.

Cathy set about cleaning the windows, which had been washed by nothing but rain since 1905. As she stood beside the back door, she noticed that her father had unfastened the lantern again.

She was annoyed, yet she found it rather touching. It was typical of him. He had done it so that, if he heard the knocking again, he could still find an excuse for it. He pretended, even to himself.

She was sure that he had been told something about this house that he didn't want them to know.

Meanwhile young Mr Stoneham, paying attention neither to Cathy nor the silver, went singlemindedly about his work. He was fast and tireless, not stopping for breaks, and by lunch-time several improvements could be seen. Cathy's mother had left her the means of making sandwiches, and when one o'clock came and he showed no sign of halting, she asked him:

"Aren't you having any lunch?"

"No, I want to get on. I'll eat proper tonight."

It was wrong for him to work so long without food, she decided. "I'm going to make you some coffee. And some sandwiches. Mummy's left me much too much."

He began to protest, but she bustled off, in charge of things. It gave her quite a warm glow, making sandwiches for him, and it pleased her to place the pile beside him, like a waitress. He made a small helpless gesture, but she bounced off again, brooking no arguments. When she went to collect his plate, she found that the sandwiches were untouched, although the coffee-mug was empty.

"Ham," he said. "I'm ever so sorry, but I'm a vegetarian."

"Oh," said Cathy.

"I'm ever so sorry. It was ever so good of–"

"I was too hasty, wasn't I? So you're a vegetarian. Are your people vegetarian?"

"People? Oh, me mum. No. My decision. I don't like animals being killed."

"You eat cheese, do you?"

21

"Oh, yes, but look miss–"

"Then I'll take out the ham and put in some cheese." And Cathy, the woman of action, hurried away again, only to return in a matter of seconds.

"I'm not doing too well as a caterer," she said. "There's about enough cheese to supply a mousetrap."

"Oh miss, it really doesn't matter–"

"Yes, it does. You shouldn't go all day without food. Look, there's a teashop place in the village. We'll both go there. All right? You'll work better with something inside you."

"You reckon?"

"Certainly I reckon. You look starved."

4

Cathy had her work cut out to get him talking. He answered her politely, volunteering nothing. She felt that he was suppressing normal high spirits, like a well-trained dog; this job of work meant a tremendous lot to him, and he was afraid of saying a word that might put it in danger. She chatted amiably, and watched him eat. After a while he loosened up. His name was Joe.

"May I call you Joe?"

"If you like, miss."

"Oh, please, not miss. Can't you manage Catherine?"

"All right, then." But he still didn't speak her name.

"Have you been working for yourself for long, Joe?"

For about eighteen months, he told her. More or less since he and his mum had been on their own. His father had been a skilled carpenter, and a general handyman besides, and Joe had learned his trade almost from infancy. When he found that he had his mother to keep he decided that it was no good working for other people at twenty-two and six a week, and so he put an ad. in the paper. Work started to come in, and he got quite a reputation by word of mouth. Nowadays he could make over four quid in a good week. This job in Polraddon was a terrific break for him. He and his mum had packed up their three rented rooms in Lewisham and taken digs in Marazion, quite cheap. It was doing his mother's health some good, too.

"Is she a widow, Joe?"

No, his father had walked out on them. He had been out of work for nearly five years and it finally got him down. Joe spoke without rancour. When you're out of work that long, you lose all self-respect. You can't love anyone, either. To love people, you need to live in comfort. People *blame* you for being out of work. They may not say so, but they do. His father grew sick of trying. He said that he wasn't going to hang around any longer, dying by inches, he'd tramp the land until he either found work or dropped dead. And that was the last they had heard of him.

"It was very hard on your mother."

"Certainly was."

"Did she take it very badly?"

"You know what she does? Every evening, around knocking-off time, she goes and stands in the street for half an hour, looking to see if he's coming back. All right," said Joe, observing Cathy's expression, "don't let it upset you. She's barmy. He wouldn't even know where we live now."

"You don't grumble at her, do you?"

"Oh no," said Joe gently, "I don't grumble at her."

Cathy looked at his eyes and saw the need to change the subject. She said, "What's made you so fond of animals?"

Well, he couldn't say. He always had been. He had a way with them. It had first made itself known when he was two years old. They were living in Deptford at that time, and one hot summer afternoon Joe's mother saw Joe lying on his back in their squalid yard with a huge rat nestling on his chest. They often saw rats in their yard, grisly brutes from the nearby sewer. Joe was

24

stroking its back. Its weak, vicious mouth was brushing his chin. She was, of course, horrified. She had been taught that rats bite your throat. She crept trembling up to the child and then suddenly shouted and stamped and flapped her apron. The rat flashed away. Joe was angry.

"Rat didn't *like* that!"

"You wicked, wicked boy," said his mother, hugging him frenetically, "it might have killed you!"

"No it wouldn't. It was a nice rat."

A few years later Joe's companions, on their scrumping expeditions, found him an invaluable ally wherever there were guard dogs. He would approach some gaunt animal, snarling up to its eyes, and hold out the back of his hand to it. The dog would close its mouth, look doubtfully at his hand, and then give in and start licking it.

"And what's the secret of that?" asked Cathy.

"You mustn't show them you're afraid of them. It stirs them up, see? Fear engenders fear."

He pronounced "engenders" with a hard "g". He had read the phrase somewhere but never heard it spoken. This charmed Cathy, for some private reason.

"And how do you manage that?"

"I dunno," he grinned.

"You ought to be a vet."

"A lot of people have said that. Think I ought to make use of my talents. It seems to me I do make use of my talents. I can make friends with any animal I like. No, I don't want to be a vet. I don't want to prove nothing. No, so long as I can make a living, I'm happy."

"On four pounds a week?"

"Make it six," he said, grinning.

In Cathy's world "getting on" was the mainspring of life. Joe was from another planet.

25

Something occurred to her. "Joe, have you ever heard of seal women?"

"Yes. Selkies."

"Oh, yes, that's right!" she exclaimed delightedly. She now remembered having heard the word somewhere. "Do you know anything about them?"

"Well, they're a legend, aren't they? Seals who turn into women. They don't never die. They live for ever."

"And never grow old, I suppose," said Cathy. "I wonder who fixes the age they stay at?"

"There's supposed to be a magic spell on them. Once a year, they shed their skins and turn into women. They can stay as women if they want to, and they even marry human men and have children and that, but it don't make them very happy, because they've always got this longing to return to the sea."

"Aren't you marvellous! How do you know all this?"

"Read about it. I've got dozens of books on animals, and some of them go in for animal legends, you know.

"If it is a legend."

"Oh well, 'course it is."

"Oh, I don't know. Shouldn't disbelieve everything you hear," said Cathy, smiling at her own wit.

"What, a seal turning into a woman!"

"The fact is, Joe, I've met one down here. I've spoken to her."

He rewarded her with a magnificent grin of incredulity.

"You don't believe me, do you?"

He continued grinning.

"All right. Just listen to this."

Her father came home in low spirits. He had hawked his paintings as far north as St Ives, and no one wanted to buy. He was too sensitive for this sort of thing.

26

"It was only to be expected," said his wife. "Down here they want pictures of fishing boats. When you've done a few of those, you'll sell them all right."

"I hope so."

"You'll see."

Although tired, she was in a curious glow of pleasure. As they ate their makeshift meal of corned beef and boiled potatoes, the reason came out.

"Guess who I met in Pendeen, Cathy. Someone you're *very* interested in."

"Bing Crosby?"

"Don't be silly, dear. A certain young man."

"*Clive*?"

"Clive Preston-Browne!"

"Whatever's he doing here?"

"Ah! I gather he *made* his mother come down. They own a cottage in Pendeen, it seems, and they've come down for–well, an indefinite period, I gather. I wonder," said Mrs Gascoyne archly, "what their motive can be, don't you?"

"Oh, Mum, didn't you gather that too?"

"What?"

"I can't answer for Clive," said Cathy, who was strangely put out at the thought of his being here, "but I'll bet that his mother is just dying to find out how we're living. She wants to gloat. Did you invite them here?"

"Well, yes." Mrs Gascoyne bisected a potato and frowningly watched the rising steam. "I've told her what to expect–this place is very run down but it has tremendous potential." She forked the potato moodily. "Oh well, she can think what she likes. I invited them for your sake."

"Thanks," said Cathy flatly.

Her mother sat ruminating over the ideas that Cathy

had just conjured up. Cathy had a terrible flair for nailing the truth.

"Don't smother your food with ketchup like that, Catherine," she said. "It looks common."

So Clive was down here. She was by no means glad of it. Still, the thought prompted her to look in the glass, and she saw, in the fading evening light, that the sea air had caused some disorder to her hair. Her neat Marcel waves had flattened somewhat and hung down limply. This made no difference whatever to her nice seventeen-year-old looks, but she thought it did, and decided to put her hair in order.

Joe had fixed up a makeshift aerial, so that they could listen to their radiogram, and at nine-thirty they switched on to a variety programme. Mabel Constanduros was on, doing one of her enormously popular Cockney monologues. "Ow, Gran'ma is a caution! She left 'er false teeth out on the windersill to cool 'em, and now the dustman's bin an' gorn and taken 'em away, and she reckons Bert's gotta run arter 'im 'n' rummidge through the dustcart to find 'em . . . Al-*fie*! Take yer 'airbrush out of the butter this *minnit*!"

Cathy compressed her lips, not nearly so amused by this as she would have been the day before, and, with a cold glance at the radiogram, went into the kitchen with her curling tongs. Her parents were relieved to see her go. The cross-talk comedians Clapham and Dwyer were on the programme, and they were sometimes rather vulgar. "I've made my will! I've written it on a hard-boiled egg!"– "A hard-boiled egg? Is that legal?"– "It's not only legal, it's binding!" It was hardly suitable for a young girl's ears.

Cathy closed the door behind her. The boom of the radio sounded through it, and then another salvo of audience laughter. How stupid it sounded, in isolation! Offensive, too. Other people's laughter antagonized you. They seemed to be on to something while you were not.

She lit the gas in the kitchen. The mantle was slightly damaged, and gave out a flickering yellow light, hissing and popping. It threw her into deep shadow when she looked in the mirror over the sink, and she could not direct the tongs accurately. She lifted the mirror from its nail and brought it over to the table, and as she turned to the centre of the room, she saw, through the newly-washed window, a face looking in at her.

She sprang back with a startled intake of breath. Then she steadied herself and cautiously approached the window. It was the face of the girl she had met on the beach, right enough. She could see the huge, black, dewy eyes, and the brown hair heavy on her shoulders. She was wrapped in the seaweed cloak, and she shone with a phosphorescent light, like a ghost.

She was an eerie night-time caller, indeed. But Cathy braced herself, unbolted the back door and opened it, and said politely in her clear voice, "I'm sorry, did you knock? I didn't hear you."

The girl moved timidly into the doorway. As the gaslight caught her, Cathy saw that she was all white from the salt of the sea. Cathy believed in rational explanations, and she was reassured to see the ghost-liness so practically accounted for. She reached out to the girl.

"Come in," she said, as winningly as she knew how. "Do come in."

The girl came into the room inch by inch, and stood and stared about her. She directed a doubtful look at the stove, where a ring was still burning, but otherwise she plainly recognized it all. She crept farther in, moving her eyes this way and that, and even feeling the wall with her hands. It was disturbing to watch her, and Cathy, despite herself, felt the goose-flesh rise on her arms.

But she was ashamed of having driven the girl off before, and was determined not to do it again. The girl knew this house. It was as if she had some ancient right to it. To be afraid of her was foolish. Joe had said, "Don't show your fear." The girl was certainly showing hers. She was trembling all over.

So Cathy smiled as hard as she could, and pointed to a chair, and said, "Sit down." And then she added–it was ludicrous, but she could think of nothing better– she added: "I'll make you a cup of tea."

The girl had stopped by the living-room door. Oh, suppose she opened it and went into the living-room itself! But she was listening to the sounds of the radio, and she looked extremely puzzled. An exchange of cross-talk was taking place, in booming tones. Cathy's parents always had it on too loud, because its volume confirmed that it was an expensive set.

There came a particularly loud cackle of laughter.

The girl jumped back, shot an accusing and terrified look at Cathy, and dashed for the outer door.

"No, wait!" cried Cathy. "It's all right! Wait, wait!"

But the girl was through the door and away. Her hair bounced on her shoulders as she ran. Cathy stumbled after her, hopelessly outpaced.

"Don't go, don't go! Wait!"

The girl ran to the very edge of the cliff. With the same lightning movement as before she threw off the cloak and somehow disposed of it. She poised there, naked and glistening in the moonlight. Stumbling, panting, catching on the gorse, Cathy struggled after her.

"Wait–*please*–"

The girl dived.

From this point on the cliff there was a sixty-foot drop. Cathy crouched down. After several seconds she heard the splash. There was a stirring of wings and a great clamour of jarring cries as hundreds of seagulls rose up to swoop round and about her very ears. She crawled fearfully to the edge and stared down. The tide was high. She could see the sickly pallor of the water at the side, and she could make out the wicked spikes of rocks.

Her mouth had gone dry. She lingered for several minutes, staring at the winking mass below, until her eyes began playing her tricks, and she fancied she could see the girl's head break the surface in place after place. She shut them tight, and when she looked again she did indeed see the leap of the white torso in a pool of moonlight.

When she regained the kitchen, the radio was still booming through the inner door, with intermittent cackling.

5

The next morning Mr Gascoyne took his sketch pad to half-way down the slope from the house and began making rough sketches of the high street of Polraddon. After half an hour or so Cathy came down to him.

"Wotcher," he said.

He liked playing the friendly dad. As a little girl, Cathy had adored him, but over the years she had grown out of him.

"Dad, I've got to talk to you."

"It'll cost you tuppence."

She sat down on the grass in front of him and leaned back on her hand, so that her straightened arm seemed to bend inward at the elbow.

"Dad, you've known all along that there was something strange about the house, haven't you? Did the agent tell you?"

"He said something or other. I didn't pay any attention."

"What did he say?"

"He didn't go into details."

"Did he say it was haunted?"

"Something of the sort."

"Is that why you got it so cheaply?"

"Maybe."

"This," said Cathy, "is like getting a tooth out. So he

said 'the house is haunted' and then stopped? He didn't tell you by what?"

"Cath, what is this?"

"*Tell* me."

"Cath, there's nothing to tell. He was very vague. He hinted at some sort of legend about the place. Why do you ask? Are you still worried about that knocking? Because—"

"Dad, listen."

She gave him an edited version of her experiences, not telling him that she had gone swimming, nor that she had invited the girl into the house. She dwelt on the girl's peculiar qualities. He listened, keeping his eye on his sketch and pretending to draw.

"A gipsy," he said at last.

"Funny sort of gipsy to live out in the Atlantic."

"But what are you trying to tell me? A seal girl? A girl who turns into a seal?"

"I didn't actually say—"

"You implied it. A seal girl! Honestly, after we've coughed up so much for your education! You put that forward as a scientific fact?"

"I've told you the facts, I don't care whether they're scientific or not."

"She's a vagrant. Living rough. Look—it's not a very nice thing to talk about, but we happen to have an outside lavatory, and she's using it. That's why she hangs around. Besides, we're worth burgling. I must get Stoneham to fix some good locks."

"Try telling that to the people in the village! Why do you think they won't come near us?"

"Well," he said slowly, after a pause, "for God's sake don't tell your mother about this. She's had enough to put up with already."

"All right, but she's bound to find out."

"Oh, I don't know. I've kept a few things from her in my time."

Cathy laughed. He really was attractive. But she persisted.

"We can't just ignore this, Dad. What do you think we should do?"

"I'd go to the police, if it weren't for frightening your mother."

"Why? How do you know this girl doesn't simply need help?"

"Oh, good God! Slinking round the house in the dead of night?"

"She's beautiful."

"*Oh . . . !*" Her father was becoming more and more agitated. It quickened his thought. "Beautiful. So are mermaids, they say. So are evil fairies. Eh? So if she's supernatural, as you seem to want to believe, she's probably a siren or something. Let her go back to the sea, if that's where she belongs. I'm sorry, I can't feel sorry for her."

"Mr Stoneham," remarked Cathy, "is even sorry for the insects behind the skirting boards. He says they've got a right there."

"Lord. What is he, a Brahmin? Well, that's very highminded of him. I believe charity begins at home."

"But you shouldn't believe it ends there. If you do you ought to give up going to church."

Mrs Preston-Browne and her son Clive called that afternoon in the Riley Nine. A Riley Nine was somewhat inferior to a Hillman, but of course much superior to no car at all. Cathy's mother had tried to arrange a picnic outing, so that they should not see the house, but her former schoolfriend was quite determined to do so, and from the rapture with which she praised it, it was plain that she was delighted with its squalor.

"Oh, *yes!*–*wonderful* bargain–*enormous* potential–Of course, it does need a *tremendous* lot done to it."

"Yes, of course," said Mrs Gascoyne, who was battling single-handed. Her husband, who hated Mrs Preston-Browne, had disappeared to paint. "We already have a little man starting on it."

"A big one, actually," said Cathy.

"I do believe we met him," said Mrs Preston-Browne. "Coming up here in a van?–yes, we asked him the way."

"Stright on up the 'ill, lidy. Yer can't miss it," said Clive.

"He doesn't speak a bit like that," said Cathy in a low voice.

"He's been sent out by a firm, has he?" asked Mrs Preston-Browne.

"No, he's on his own."

"Oh, one of these little backdoor oddjobbers. I should watch him if I were you."

"He seems reliable enough," said Mrs Gascoyne uneasily.

"Yes, but sometimes these people are working for a gang. They take stock of your belongings and let their accomplices in when the time is ripe. But still, no doubt I'm doing him an injustice. It's to his credit that he's found work, anyway. It's proven fact that most of the unemployed just don't want work–"

Mrs Preston-Browne realized just too late that she had put her foot in it, and covered her confusion with a barrage of words.

"Of course, of course, I'm speaking of the lower classes. The trouble is, far too much is done for them nowadays, and they just take advantage. The fact is they actually *prefer* to live in slums. It's a proven fact.

35

These council houses–well, you wouldn't believe the tales you hear. Tell them about the council estate near you, darling."

"There's one near the school," said Clive. "We have clashes with the louts, sometimes. Yes, some of the people who've moved in there have never seen a bathroom. They've started keeping their coal in the baths."

"And they'll break their windows, you know, and then patch them with brown paper," said Mrs Preston-Browne. "They simply *want* to–"

Cathy said quietly, "Excuse me," and walked out of the room.

Her mother glanced after her, unperturbed.

"Clive," she said, after having discreetly ascertained that Cathy had not merely gone out in quest of the lavatory, "I think that may have been a signal."

"Nothing like making yourself plain." said Mrs Preston-Browne, who had qualms, now that the Gascoynes were poor, about Cathy's worthiness for her son. But Clive rose up, with his easy smile, and strolled out.

He found Cathy sitting on the stone wall in front of the house.

"Mind if I join you?"

"Yes, I do."

"I don't follow you," said Clive, in well-mannered puzzlement.

"Good. Please don't."

"I say, what?"

"I wish to be sick."

"Oh, rotten luck," said Clive automatically.

"Can't you do anything better than squawk your silly stock phrases like a stupid parrot? No, it's not rotten luck, as it happens. It's rotten *talk*. Yours. Do you know how *disgusting* you all sounded in there?"

"I simply don't understand."

"No, and you wouldn't in a million years. Go away, if you don't want me to throw up all over you."

She hurried away. She began weeping as she went. Clive stood there, nonplussed, for several moments, his shapely mouth slightly open. But then his worldly wisdom came to his aid. Girls commonly went mad at certain times of the month, didn't they? Satisfied with this, he strolled back to the house.

Joe was climbing into his van when Cathy, tear-stained, her hair more blown about than ever, stumbled into him.

"Marvellous, isn't it?" he said. "That's twice I've been into the town for putty, and each time they've said come back in an hour."

"Let me come with you."

He looked uncertain.

"Please."

Without a word he came round and opened the passenger door for her. They drove out of the village and into the next town in silence. He drew in to the kerb.

"Where d'you want to go, then?"

"Nowhere."

He turned to look at her. "Been listening to some sad records, have you?"

"I'm upset, Joe."

"So I see." Without further comment he left the car to go into a shop. He came back with a tin and pulled the starting handle from under the driving seat.

"Joe, wait."

Joe waited.

"I'm furious," said Cathy, in a rush. "My disgusting

mother has got some disgusting visitors and their talk was so disgusting that I just got up and walked out. Honestly, the snobbery! 'The lowah clahsses always put their coals in the bahth, my deah!' That's Mrs Preston-Browne, for your information. She thinks you might be doing a reconnaissance for a team of burglars! I wanted to be sick, I just got up and walked out."

"I wish you hadn't."

"I shouldn't have told you. I've offended you," said Cathy, in dismay.

"No, but I wish you hadn't walked out. You can always walk *back*, and they've got to have you. They can kick me out. They can say what they like, it's no skin off my nose, but this job is a big one for me and I don't want to lose it."

Cathy's face clearly showed that she thought she deserved more gratitude. "All right," said Joe, "it was nice of you to get angry over me, but you just don't know you're born, do you? Do you know what it's like to lose a job?"

"Yes, actually. My dad happens to be out of work at present, and you are not."

"He's out of work in a very cosy world, he is. Blind ole Reilly! He's paying me nigh on sixty quid for this job! Do you think they could get that sort of money where I come from? One week my mum had sixpence in her purse. Sixpence in the whole world. You want to know what it's like to hang around a crowd of people hoping they'll offer you a cigarette, or call on someone deliberate, choosing your time, because you think they'll be making a pot of tea? Your dad don't know he's born."

"I'm sorry," said Cathy, forlornly.

He relented. "Proper told you off, haven't I?"

"Yes, haven't you just. It'll be a wonder if I don't get

an inferiority complex before long. I'm getting rejected all round. First it's the villagers, who treat us as though we were lepers, then it's the seal girl, now it's you."

"No, steady on, this seal girl, as you call her, she didn't reject you, I reckon you rejected her."

"No, there have been further developments."

She told him of last night's visit.

"Frightened off by the laughter," he mused. "Now why should she be that? Some dogs hate laughter. Like, if a dog had a tin can tied to its tail when it was a puppy, it'll hate being laughed at, it'll remember people jeering at it, you see."

"This wasn't jeering laughter, just rather silly."

"Yes, but she wasn't to know that. I reckon some-one's laughed at her some time. Blimey, she's a funny sort of girl, isn't she? Weren't you a bit scared of her?"

"To be honest, she gave me the creeps."

"You asked her into your house, though."

"The problem is keeping her there! She keeps coming back to it, but she runs and hides for the slightest reason."

"Why do you bother about her, Catherine?"

(Catherine!) "She's lonely," said Cathy.

"I like you," said Joe.

"Joe, that's made my day. Why?"

"You worry about other people."

"Oh, Joe, what a pious reason for liking me! Nothing else?"

His eyes twinkled. "Well, you talk posh. You're a lady."

Cathy laughed. She had a fine, ringing laugh.

"Not all the time I'm not," she said.

6

"You have disgraced me, Catherine," said Mrs Gascoyne in a vibrating voice. "You've made me a laughing-stock. Can't you see that woman rushing round to tell everyone?"

"Does it matter what she says?"

"It may not to you but it does to me. You were abominably rude. You walked out on our visitors before our very eyes, you insulted Clive, and the next thing we know, you're driving off in a commercial van with Stoneham. Whatever next?"

"What difference does it make that the van was commercial?"

"Catherine, don't be impertinent. I want to know whatever made you do it."

"Mrs Preston-Browne's revolting snobbery."

"And who are you to judge your elders? In any case," demanded Mrs Gascoyne, as suspicions flared up, "why should you suddenly become so touchy about that? Catherine? Catherine, answer me?"

Cathy stared silently back.

"It's Stoneham, isn't it?" said her mother, shaking.

Cathy did not answer.

"Well, you don't have to say it. You've been running after that fellow ever since he came. A common labourer! And then to go off with him in a van! You

40

don't know what harm might have come to you."

"As a matter of fact," said Cathy, "he quite literally wouldn't hurt a fly. He happens to be a strict vegetarian."

"Oh, you have learned a lot about him, haven't you? And are you telling me that young girls are safe with vegetarians? Because if so you must be exceedingly naive."

"This is a ridiculous conversation," said Cathy languidly.

"Catherine, don't make me lose my temper or you'll be sorry for it. Admit it, now, you are infatuated with this workman, aren't you?"

"I respect him," said Cathy cautiously. "I think he's got a lot of courage, starting up a business of his own. I also think he has very high principles. Between ourselves, if you're worried about harm coming to me, you want to think a bit about Clive. He can be quite a naughty boy, Clive. Whereas Joe—"

Mrs Gascoyne pounced on this.

"So it's Joe, is it?" she cried. "We've got that far, have we? Joe!" She spoke the name as if she were holding a dirty rag at arm's length. "And his brothers are named Alf and Sid, I suppose? *Joe!*"

"It was a good enough name for the father of Christ," said Cathy.

"Catherine, how dare you! I will not tolerate blasphemy! Well, *Joe* isn't going to remain here for another minute, and he's got you to thank for it."

In the silence that followed, Joe could just be heard, working outside at the back. He must have much more than "just" heard Mrs Gascoyne. She lowered her voice, snapping.

"Your father shall dismiss him as soon as he gets back."

Cathy kept calm, although she was afraid for Joe. She knew her father's position, and she knew in advance what he would say.

"He's an excellent workman, and he's half the price of the others."

"If you won't, I will."

"We can't afford it."

Money ruled. Mrs Gascoyne sulked for a while. Then: "Catherine, you are neither to see him nor to speak to him again. Is that understood?"

"Yes, all right."

"You are quite sure?"

"Oh, yes."

It was an order which, they both knew, could not possibly be enforced. Mrs Gascoyne was really helpless, and Cathy felt pity for her creeping in, but she kept her counsel. She had already formulated a plan.

If her mother had not made so much of it, she might well have abandoned the pursuit of Joe of her own accord. There didn't seem to be much future in it. But her mother had used the one way of hardening her resolve.

Her plan was drastic. Feeling wicked, and enjoying it, albeit shakily, Cathy wrote a note to Joe. *Meet me Lower Cliff Road 8 o'clock? Nod if yes. Catherine.* Then she went out to the lavatory. (What service it was doing! She thought of a joke: "I never thought that outside W.C. would prove such a convenience!" and hoped that Joe would find it funny.) As she went, she slipped him the note. On the way back, she was trembling so much that her knees would hardly hold her up. Joe glanced at her dispassionately, but he did give the briefest nod, and Cathy went back to the house in elation.

Now for Clive.

This was the wicked bit. She was about to play a dirty

trick on Clive. Not cricket, as he would say. Well, she had been driven to it. And, all things considered, he deserved it. Thus she fought with her conscience. Her conscience put up a game struggle, but she won.

By good fortune, the Preston-Brownes' cottage in Pendeen was on the telephone, and Mrs Gascoyne, Clive's publicity manager, had roundly made the number known, but as Cathy entered the telephone box in the village, the ramshackle nature of her plan struck her. Suppose Clive were going out tonight? Or refused to see her? Suppose his ghastly mother answered the phone? Yes, that was more than likely; she must be ready for it. She rehearsed a meek, faltering speech in her head. "May I–may I speak to Clive please?" But as it happened, Clive himself answered.

"Oh, hallo!" To her relief, he seemed pleased.

"Clive, will you come and see me this evening?" (Oh, suppose that damned woman wanted the Riley Nine for herself?)

"Yes, all right."

(Thank goodness.) "About seven o'clock, then?"

"All right."

"Make it *exactly* seven o'clock."

"Yes, all right."

"You won't be late, will you?"

"No, all right. I say, Cath, what's on?"

"Tell you when I see you."

"Oh, all right. Jolly good."

He sounded jubilant. She really was treating him badly. "All's fair in love and war," she told herself. All the same . . .

Mrs Gascoyne was still hardly speaking to Cathy, but over the evening meal, which they always ate early, at about six o'clock, Cathy let slip the fact that Clive was calling, and her mother's anger swiftly subsided, as a

43

howling baby's will when a sweet is thrust under its nose.

"I wonder he wants to see you, after the way you treated him."

"We didn't quarrel, Mum."

"He must be a very patient boy, then." But Mrs Gascoyne was mollified. "You are going out with him, are you?"

"Yes."

"What are you going to do?"

"Really, dear," said her husband reproachfully.

"Perhaps that was a tactless question." She smiled, pleased with the thoughts it conjured up. She admired Clive because he represented status, and condoned in him what she would have condemned in others. "Well, not too late back now. Half-past ten? All right?"

The daring of her plan made Cathy weak. As seven o'clock drew near, she hovered about the windows in the front, almost sick with excitement. But Clive always kept his word. Exactly on the hour the Riley Nine drew up some twenty yards below–parking was difficult higher up–and he got out. He was wearing very pale flannels which flapped over his toe-caps, a striped blazer, and a cream shirt open at the neck with a silk cravat of Paisley design inside it. His forehead and cheeks had caught the sun. He looked irresistible. He strolled up the slope with his long, easy stride, as if he were favouring the earth by walking on it.

Mrs Gascoyne took Cathy by the elbow and drew her away. "Come on. It doesn't do to look too eager. Go and powder your nose. I'll talk to Clive."

By five past seven they were in the car. Cathy made Clive drive to a strip of common a little way out of the village, where there was no danger of encountering Joe on his way in. His face brightened when he noted all the gorse bushes, the heather, and the solitude, and he made to get out of the car.

"No, wait, Clive. Clive . . . we're good friends, aren't we?"

"Yes, rather."

"Yes. Well, Clive . . . Clive, I'm going to ask you to do me a hell of a favour."

"Go on, then."

"Clive, I . . . Clive, look. There's someone I very, very much want to see. This evening, Clive. And my mother is dead against my seeing him. And I . . . I want you to let me say I've been out with you. Putting it bluntly, that's it, Clive."

While she was speaking, Clive's face underwent a change, and when she spoke the word "him", his eyes filled with pain. He went very red, and for a terrible moment she thought he was going to cry. She was appalled. She had never dreamed he would take it like this. He cuddled her whenever he got the chance, of course, and she didn't mind, for he was an attractive boy, but as for having any real affection for her as a person—no! He *enjoyed* her, as if she were a chocolate eclair.

"Clive," she protested, "we have never been any more than friends, have we?"

"That's what you think," he said bitterly.

"Oh, Clive, be fair! You wouldn't even come and see me off when we moved! What was I supposed to think?"

"I came down here, didn't I?"

She had no answer to that. She surreptitiously glanced at her watch. Twenty-five past.

"Someone you've met down here, is it?" he demanded sullenly.

She nodded.

45

"Older man, is he?"

"Well, yes."

She had been dreading the moment when he would guess it was Joe, but some mythical "older man" filled his mind.

"You be jolly careful," he muttered.

"What of, Clive?"

"Just be careful, that's all," he repeated darkly.

"Clive, I didn't dream it would upset you like this. I'm honestly sorry."

"I am not upset," he retorted, flushed and shaking.

"You did, sort of, seem it, actually."

"Nothing of the kind."

It was half past seven.

"You want me to go, I suppose?"

She was conscience stricken.

"Oh, what will you do for the rest of the evening?"

"Pictures, I suppose."

"There's Fred Astaire and Ginger Rogers in *The Gay Divorce*. It's supposed to be very good," she said, inanely.

"I expect I'll enjoy myself no end."

He got out of the car and held the door open for her. She felt she could not grovel enough, but it would do no good, and besides, time was going on.

"Clive, this *is* between ourselves, isn't it?"

It gave him the perfect exit line. "One does not tell tales, " he said icily.

"It's jolly decent of you, Clive."

"Thank you. Good-night."

And he drove away, in a mood to leave for darkest Africa and shoot big game.

It was a long walk to the lower cliff road, and Cathy was out of breath when she reached it. Joe was there, sitting at the wheel of his van. He had changed from his overalls, and was wearing a neat charcoal-blue suit, almost certainly from the Fifty Shilling Tailors. The sight of him dressed up for her swept away all other feelings. She scrambled up beside him, turning to him so eagerly that to take her in his arms would have seemed a matter of course. He looked at her severely.

"So what's it about, then?"

What could one possibly answer to that?

"I wanted to see you."

He frowned. "Look, your mother has been watching me all day long. She's kept coming out, pretending she was looking for something. Keeping an eye on me, she was."

"Why did you come, Joe?" she asked despairingly.

"I suppose I was curious. Does your mother know you're meeting me?"

"No." Oh, this was difficult. She could not tell him the half of it.

In fact, she could not tell him any of it. She realized that she had misjudged him as badly as she had misjudged Clive. She had built her hopes on the strength of one speech of his. "I like you." She had repeated it to herself a hundred times. He had meant what he had said, no more.

She hoped that they would laugh together over the framing of Clive, making a guilty joke of it. You can get away with many a dirty trick if you make it seem funny enough. But Joe was not in a mood for jokes. He was tense and worried.

Everything had gone wrong.

She contrived some halting story. She left Clive out of it altogether. Her mother she mentioned only obliquely. But Joe caught on.

"I've half killed myself setting myself up. I'm doing all right, working, earning a living. Your dad likes my

47

work. I don't want it all mucked up."

"No, of course you don't," she said wretchedly.

There was a silence so extremely long that Cathy dolefully considered getting up and walking away, but at last he muttered:

"I suppose I seem selfish."

"No. You've got your mother to think of, haven't you?"

"Yes, right," he said, and seemed mildly surprised that she should be so perceptive.

Quite self-possessed, Cathy said, "We'd better break this up, hadn't we?"

"Afraid so, girl. I can't afford to play around."

"I mustn't be seen with you. I'll walk back up the cliff path."

"I'll come with you nearly to the top."

They left the lower cliff road and walked along the sands to where the cliff path began. He went ahead of her up the path. Now and then he gave her a helping hand, but as formally as a conductor helping an old lady off a bus.

"Just wait a minute," she said. He stopped, obedient as the milkman's horse. "Let's just watch the sea for a while. They'll ask questions if I get back too early."

Cathy began crying quietly. Looking out to sea, he did not notice. She blew her nose and recovered herself. She glanced sideways at him. He wouldn't notice if she jumped over the cliff, she thought. But she was glad he hadn't seen her tears. They were unfair, a kind of blackmail. She had no right to burden him with her emotions. Oh, but he was hard to reach. He was as bad as the seal girl. She turned back to the sea.

She said suddenly, "Look!"

The tide was coming in, in low, white, parallel rollers. A hundred yards out a sleek head could be seen, looking like a silver ball in the evening sun.

"It's a seal," said Joe.

"Yes," she said, disappointed.

In fact there were several of them, moving leisurely towards the shore. Three came clear of the water and flopped their luscious bodies a little way up the sand, to sink down and flatten out their noses like dogs.

"They're beautiful," said Joe reverently. "They're–"

But she interrupted. "There! Look!"

There were more seals in the water. But just beyond them the girl had come into view, head on to the shore, advancing in that leaping charge of hers, racing past the seals themselves. And then the deep dive down.

"Stone a crow," said Joe hoarsely, fascinated.

"I should have thought you'd be against stoning crows," said Cathy. "Now do you believe me?"

"That's wonderful," said Joe, in the same rapt, hoarse tones.

"Didn't I tell you?"

"Sh'sh."

He knelt down, and Cathy knelt beside him, sitting on her heels and fanning out her white skirt round her. She did not dare speak to him again. His gaze was riveted on the sea. They stayed thus for long minutes.

"Isn't she never going to come up again?" said Joe.

After a period impossibly long for any normal human being, the girl emerged at the edge, shining and streaming. She shook her magnificent head, flinging off the drops in fiery rain, and dropped down on the sand among the seals. She straightened her arms and arched her back and looked skyward, It was the seal attitude. A shiver ran through Cathy.

"*Selkie*", she said, under her breath.

"What will she do, do you suppose?"

"She'll make for our house, I expect."

"She won't get much of a welcome there!"

"She'll have to come this way. We might be able to speak to her."

After a while the girl rose, and went behind the rock from which Cathy had first seen her. When she came into sight again she had her seaweed cloak wrapped round her. Slowly and cautiously, as if in fear of an ambush, she began creeping up the beach.

"I'm going down," said Joe.

"Don't frighten her, Joe."

"Don't worry."

He went swiftly down the cliff path. The girl spotted him and turned to a statue, glistening weirdly in the dying light. Joe disappeared under the overhang of the cliff for a while, and when he reappeared Cathy saw that he was not making for the girl, but for the three seals, who were still lying sleek, complacent and unperturbed by the edge of the water. Steadily, easily, Joe walked to meet them. All the tension had gone out of him. Cathy could sense his quiet assurance even from where she was. She heard the light even crunch of his feet on the sand. The seals reared up on their flippers and pointed their noses as if about to do circus tricks. Joe squatted in front of them and appeared to be talking to them. They sank down between their flippers again as if under massage. They mooned at him like contented cats. He edged forward and stroked the foremost one on the top of its head, and then under its chin, near its dangerous teeth.

The girl stood still, but uncertainly now, with a new attentiveness. Joe rose up and began to walk towards her. He got right up to her and reached out to take her arm, with all the confidence of a man unlocking his own front door.

The girl suddenly made up her mind. She sprang

back, whipped off the cloak and disposed of it bewilderingly, like a conjuror, and with a few astonishing bounds threw herself into the water. The seals, a few yards away, turned and flopped back after her. Joe watched her receding head for a few moments. Then he turned in defeat and walked back up the beach.

7

Joe knelt beside Cathy and put his arm round her shoulders, but in a distracted way, while still gazing out at sea, where the girl and her seals had now sunk without trace.

"Didn't work, did it?"

Cathy leaned her head against the fifty shilling suit. "You certainly have a way with animals, Joe. Perhaps not with girls."

"She's a rum sort of girl," he said, smiling ruefully.

"Beautiful, though."

"Oh, yes. I never seen anything like her."

"Love at first sight, was it?"

"You know what? I was scared. I might not have shown it, but I was trembling from head to foot. Yes," said Joe, "of course, that was it. She sensed it. Smelt my fear. Like an animal."

"She's a selkie."

"It's amazing," muttered Joe, shaking his head. "Amazing. She's animal, and yet more than human."

"That's clever, Joe. What's it mean?"

"I don't know," he said. "It's just something I feel."

"Well," said Cathy, "it's not just the smell of your fear that frightens her. I never saw anyone so nervous. The least thing scares her. And everyone's scared of her in turn. It's ridiculous."

"I can understand the villagers being scared of her."

"So can I. But I keep reminding myself, she saved my life."

"I think you'd take her side in any case," said Joe. "You've got a soft spot for people who are down on their luck, you have. You're all for the underdog."

"Oh, am I, Joe? Yes, perhaps I am. Perhaps I think underdogs so much nicer than overdogs. Not to mention overbitches. Anyway, you're agreed that she *is* a seal girl, are you? You don't believe that stuff about her being a gipsy or a wild girl or something?"

"I agree with you," said Joe. "I reckon everyone has to, in the end."

"Yes, because I'm always right."

"You all right now? Shall we go on up?"

"No, don't let's move just yet, m'm?"

For answer he took her by the shoulders and very gently pushed her upright.

"Oh, my God," she said, "I'm throwing myself at you, aren't I?"

He gazed at her for a long time, as though hesitating over something in a shop window which he knew was beyond his means. He shook his head ever so slightly. "Come on," he said. "Let's walk to the top."

Cathy picked her way cautiously through the garden and let herself in at the front of the house. She had come home early. They were likely to ask questions. How tiresome. But there would be no avoiding it. She held her head up, and marched into the living room.

Their expressions were grim, and for an awful moment she thought they had found out about this evening, but her mother's first words dispelled her fears.

"Back rather early, dear?"

53

"I didn't want you to worry about me," said Cathy hypocritically. "Mum—is anything wrong?"

"We've had a visit from the Vicar."

"The Pendeen one?"

"No, the local one. It seems that the villagers are complaining about this house being occupied. They say it brings bad luck. It stops them catching fish. If ever you heard such—"

"Even I know that fish can't be caught in calm water," chimed in her father, "and the sea's been like a millpond lately."

Cathy caught his eye for a moment. "How does this house come into it?"

"Ask your father," said her mother.

"He wouldn't come in," said her father. "He took me outside for a chat. He's as scared as the silly villagers."

"But what . . . ?"

"He wouldn't go into details." Mr Gascoyne began rather feverishly impersonating the Vicar. "'Not that I—ah—sub*scraibe* to this supahstition, but we—ah—have to keep the village folk happeigh, ha-ha-ha!'"

"What superstition?"

"That's what we can't make out," said her mother.

"What are we supposed to do?"

"He wants us to leave this house, if you please," said her mother.

"You won't will you?" demanded Cathy, paling.

"Of course not. Out of the question," said her father. "It seems there's a cottage at the other end of the village. He thinks I should move there."

"And own two houses? He's mad."

"He's frightened," said her mother. "He ought to be ashamed of himself, an educated man."

But the Vicar, thought Cathy, had told her father a lot more than her father had told them. She was determined to tackle him as soon as she could get him alone.

"Let's have it, then, Dad."
He was expecting her. He was only pretending to paint.
"Can't keep anything from you, can I?"
He attempted a laugh, and she felt sorry for him. She did something unusual for her. She took his hands, and, kneeling on the grass in front of him, held them in her lap.
"Tell me."
"It's nonsense. It's about a legend."
"Yes?"
"Well . . ."

Well. The legend concerned a young man named John Tregarthen, and it had begun a hundred and twenty years ago.

He was, of course, a fisherman, and a native of Polraddon: a solitary young man who seemed to like the company of the seagulls better than that of human beings, for he built a small hut on the height of the cliff, out by itself, where he dwelt alone and made a scanty living.

The tiny bay below the cliff was a gathering place for seals. He often saw them sunbathing on the shore, and he would have liked to make friends with them, but seals are shy of men.

One day, when he was walking on the shore, he heard the sound of singing from behind some rocks. He crept to the rocks and peered over, but by this time the singing had ceased, and there was no one there to account for it. Lying about the shore, however, were several seal-skins, grey, black, and golden-brown.

They belonged to the selkies, that family of sisters

55

who had lived under the waves until, countless ages ago, they had been turned to seals by the spell of a sea-witch. The spell allowed them to shed their skins and turn back into women once a year. Having done this, they could keep their human form until such time as they chose to reclaim their skins. But, in all the enormous family, throughout the ages, only a very few had elected to live on land for longer than the one day in the year, and those that had done so had ended in sorrow.

All this John Tregarthen did not know, for very rarely did the selkies leave their skins in the sight of mortal men. He picked up one skin, golden-brown and silky, and hid it in his hut.

It belonged to a selkie named Fiona, the most beautiful of all the myriad beauties of her clan. When the time came for her and her sisters to don their skins again and return to the sea, Fiona found herself stranded in the treacherous world of the land. She made her way to John Tregarthen's hut and knocked on the door. So innocent was she that she did not think of covering herself, and so John Tregarthen opened his door on a girl of extraordinary loveliness, clad only in her own long, lustrous brown hair.

"Help me, sir. I am a daughter of the sea. Until I find my seal-skin, I cannot rejoin my sisters."

He did not understand her words, because she spoke in the ancient language of the sea, but he guessed what they meant. But as soon as he set eyes on Fiona, he fell helplessly in love with her, and so, instead of giving her back her skin, he pretended not to understand what she wanted. He drew her gently into the hut, and wrapped her in a shawl, and brought her food, and waited on her tenderly.

From that time on they lived together as man and

wife. At first, Fiona stayed only because she hoped to find her seal skin in these parts. The call of the sea was still strong. But the power of human love is greater than any other–

(At this, Cathy raised her eyebrows and said, "Oh, it is, is it?"

"So they say," replied her father lightly, and went on with the story.)

John Tregarthen was so good to Fiona that after a while she returned his love. She learned his language, and shared his work, and was so happy that she lost her desire to return to the sea, although she remained a wonderful swimmer, and would take to the treacherous water and swim great distances without feeling cold or fatigue. And, mysteriously, their union brought him luck. He seemed only to wish the fish into his nets to bring them home in shoals. He became prosperous, and employed other men to develop his trade. No longer content with his hut, he had it pulled down and replaced with a spacious three-bedroomed house, and continued to prosper.

But the villagers were jealous of him. And their wives hated Fiona. They hated her unageing beauty. They hated her happiness. They objected to her swimming naked, which they said was immoral. They suspected that she was not legally married, which was also immoral. Above all, they hated her for "a foreigner", because, although Fiona had been native to their shores for an immeasurably longer time than themselves, they regarded anyone who had not been born in the streets of the village as foreign. Gradually, in the course of village gossip, they got out of John Tregarthen the full story of his mysterious bride, and they gave his happiness and prosperity an evil interpretation. They spread the rumour that Fiona had bewitched the waters, so that her husband got all the fish that their husbands should be getting. And finally, they drove her away.

"How?" asked Cathy.

"The Vicar wouldn't say. No, honestly–he avoided that question. I gather that they did something that upset her so much that she rushed into the sea and swam out, and was not seen again in their lifetime."

"Poor thing."

"It worked, though, didn't it?"

"What happened to John Tregarthen?"

"It seems that he died of a broken heart. He left a curse on this village. And now legend has it that if ever the house is occupied, the selkie will return, and the fishing trade will be ruined."

"Other people have lived in it, though."

"Yes, two or three times, and each time, according to report, she's been spotted, and trade has been bad. Well, that's the tale, darling. Now don't you admit it's preposterous? A seal woman! This is the twentieth century."

"Doesn't the twentieth century bother about evidence?"

"There must be a rational explanation of the girl you keep seeing."

"Yes, it's that she's really and truly a selkie."

"I just can't talk you out of this, can I?"

"No, and you'll have to convince a lot more people than me."

"I know. I wouldn't try reasoning with villagers. I asked the Vicar if there wasn't some exorcism mumbo-jumbo he could perform to keep them quiet. He didn't take too kindly to that. 'Ay don't approve of–ah–meddling with the supahnatural.' But all the same, he wants me to leave the house and take the cottage. And the fact is, I damn well can't."

Cathy crept round to the side of the house, to where Joe had now shifted—and where her mother couldn't see them—and drew, with her finger, a figure eight in the dust at his feet. With a slight motion of her thumb she indicated the direction of the lower cliff road. She raised questioning eyebrows.

Joe was singing quietly.

"Sweet *a-a-and* love-lee,
Sweeter than the roses in May . . ."

Without interrupting his song he nodded briefly, and winked, putting Cathy in a flutter, which lasted all day, as to what was making him so happy.

"Out with Clive again?" said her mother that evening.

"Yes, Mum."

"He hasn't come in the car this time?"

"No, his mother's using it." Awful, how glibly the lies came now!

Cathy climbed up beside Joe in the van.

"You look pleased about something."

"Yes, we've had a letter from my dad. He's found where we are. He's got a job, and wants us to join him."

"Oh!" said Cathy, as her edifice of foolish hopes collapsed. "And will you join him?"

"Not till I've finished the job on your house, naturally. After that, I don't know. But Mum will. She's overjoyed."

"Oh," said Cathy. Then, cordially. "Oh, I'm so glad for you, Joe. And your mother." And as she smiled she hated Joe's father and his mother, for being the cause of his happiness.

And then she felt ashamed of herself for hating them,

and so she deliberately kept on questioning him, at first only as a kind of penance, but then with growing interest.

"What sort of job has he got?"

"Storekeeper in a timber yard in New Cross. It's not much of a job. Two pound ten a week. But he sounds as pleased as a dog with two tails."

"He won't be using his talents."

"Oh no, he's a skilled craftsman, but that's the way it is these days. Think yourself lucky to get anything."

"Joe," said Cathy, "write to your father."

"Oh, Mum's done that, you bet."

"Yes, but you write, too. Ask him to join you in your business."

Joe's eyes widened. "You don't half think of some things," he said.

"I'm surprised you haven't thought of it yourself. While you're doing a big job like the house, you must be losing quite a bit of work, because you can't be in two places at once. After you'd got started, you could double your income."

"You don't know my old man. He's a pig-headed so-and-so, very touchy. He'd blow his top if I asked him to work for me."

"Then be diplomatic, Joe. Say you need his advice and his experience and all that. Make it sound as if you'll be working for him. Stoneham and Son. We all know it'll be Stoneham and Father, but what does it matter? Joe, this timber yard job is an insult. You could give him back his self-respect."

Joe put his elbow on his knee and his cheek on his fist and looked like Rodin's Thinker.

"That letter would take some writing," he said.

"I'll help you with it."

"Would you?"

"Yes, of course. So that's all right, then," said Cathy, as if making a tick mentally. "Now, then–"

"So that's all right, then" echoed Joe, faintly. "Stone a bleeding crow."

"Listen–"

And she related the legend of the selkie.

"Fiona," she said.

"Yes," said Joe, almost reluctantly, "that's her, all right."

"It's a romantic story, isn't it?"

"No, it's a rotten story. That John Whatsisname must have been a right selfish so-and-so."

"He was in love with her."

"Meaning, he wanted to go to bed with her."

"I've always thought there was some connection," said Cathy mildly.

"If he'd have really loved her he would have given her her freedom. He'd have chanced it whether she stayed with him or not. I expect she quite liked being pampered for a bit, but I bet that deep down inside her she bore him the hell of a grudge. That's typical of human beings," said Joe. "Everything under the sun has got to be arranged for their pleasure. Like, with animals, they either bloody kill them or else they shut them up in zoos or teach them circus tricks. No, I do not go a bundle on John Thingummy. Selfish."

"Yes, I see what you mean," said Cathy, impressed. "Well, you can see why she keeps going back to the house, can't you?"

"Looking for her skin."

"That's right."

"He probably cut it into strips or buried it somewhere miles away."

"No, I don't think so. I don't think he would have destroyed it, for fear of destroying her with it. I think he hid it in the house somewhere."

"So why does she only go to the house when it's occupied? It would be easier when it was empty."

"I don't know," said Cathy, rather crossly.

"Blimey, so there's something you don't know, is there?" said Joe, grinning. "Well! I'm the man for this situation, aren't I, because I'm practically taking your house to pieces."

"Yes, Joe, you are. And if you could help the selkie, you'd be helping my dad, too."

"Yes," said Joe thoughtfully, "he's in a right state of jitters, isn't he? So that's why, is it? I don't know where I'm going to start looking, though."

"Oh, anywhere and everywhere, nowhere in particular," said Cathy. "But get your letter written, Joe. First things first."

"O.K.," said Joe. He seemed slightly dazed.

8

Clive Preston-Browne had never dreamed that Cathy would look at anyone else. She was one of his certainties. It was not that he took her lightly. He daydreamed about her all the time, but he never told her his feelings; he couldn't; he would have felt an ass. He had been schooled to conceal his emotions. Nevertheless they were there. He assumed she knew.

And now it was the end of the world. The thought of Cathy's eyes, and her hair, and her lips, and her voice, and her body in its summer dress which the wind blew into outlines, tormented him without relief.

He took to going for long walks, his shoulders hunched, his hands deep in his pockets, his eyes burning the ground: the wronged hero. Partly, let it be admitted, he did so to get away from his mother.

"She's no great catch, you know. The Gascoynes really are disgracefully poor. Wait a year or two and you'll do much better for yourself."

"Mother, you'll make me very angry."

She was somewhat in awe of him. She and her husband had devoted themselves to giving him "advantages", and these, of course, had raised him to a higher class. All the same, he was her product, and Cathy's lure for him rankled.

Clive's feet would lead him, inexorably, towards

Polraddon. He hoped all the time that he would meet her by accident, but he never did. He would stride through the village and up the hill till he was within hailing distance of Cathy's house, and then some complex of pride and uncertainty would stop him from calling on her, and he would trek round it, and tramp down the cliff path to the beach.

He watched the sea, and was torn by thoughts just as ungovernable. He imagined Cathy's new lover, the Older Man she had met down here. A visitor on holiday. Girls were easy victims of holiday romances. He would be experienced, debonair, and, of course, a bounder. He would have a slim black moustache. Clive always pictured him in evening dress, even though it would be singularly out of place on the Cornish holiday coast. He saw the two of them in settings which were also seldom found in these villages—cafes with candlelight and romantic music, where they sipped wine and murmured enchantments. And the foolish girl would be lapping it up, unwary of the danger she was in.

Or (God!) was she actually *loose*? You could never tell with women. The best of them were corruptible.

Thinking in this vein, Clive worked himself into a boiling rage. Then his mood changed, and he was ashamed of his suspicions. Cathy wasn't like that. She was a jolly decent girl. She needed protecting. Oh, why couldn't she see that he was the one to protect her? . . .

He turned away from the barren, barren shore, and began to climb the cliff path. Like some mechanism that goes into reverse at intervals, his mood changed back from sentimental to furious, and he drove himself up the path with savage thrusts of his thighs. When the roof of Cathy's house came in sight he halted, and, being too spent for further rage, was overcome with dejection.

He gazed at the beach below. The tide was coming in, and now the water heaved a little. The sea here, they said, was treacherous. He thought of wading in and swimming out till he drowned. He would leave a note for Cathy with his clothes on some ledge of the cliff. He composed it in his head, with variations. Sometimes it was bitter, sometimes piteous. The trouble was, it wouldn't be worth his while dying and leaving a note unless he could live to see its effect on her.

Suddenly he flushed, his heart pounded, he began shaking all over. A girl and a man were walking on the sands. The girl looked like Cathy. As they drew nearer he saw that it *was* Cathy, her skirt fluttering deliciously in the breeze. The Older Man was tall and dark.

And now Clive saw who he was, and the debonair seducer of his fancy vanished.

His flush faded until he became quite white. He was deeply shocked.

Angry and wretched, he watched for them to kiss, embrace, or show any amorous signs. They did not. They were not even hand in hand, but walked slowly with their heads down, apparently deep in talk. A nun pacing with her confessor would not have looked more demure.

They began to ascend the cliff path. Clive could not move. And so they came upon him.

"Clive!!"

He gave them a wild stare. Then he muttered "Excuse me," and hurried away. He shuddered as he went, as if fleeing from an abomination.

"He'll go and tell everybody he's seen us," said Joe resignedly.

"No, not Clive."

"Why are you so sure?"

"It's something he'd never do."

"Your boy-friend, is he?"

"That's what he thinks, but I happen not to agree."

"He's crazy about you, anyway."

"I don't know, is he? You've decided that pretty quickly, haven't you?"

"You can see that a mile off. Oh, yes. Jealousy written all over him. And disgust. He thinks it terrible that you should be going around with a feller that drops his aitches."

"You don't drop your aitches."

"You know what I mean."

"All right, if you say so. I can assure you of one thing, though, Joe—you understand a lot of things, but you don't understand Clive if you think he'd tell tales on someone."

"Well, I hope you're right. All I know is, I don't trust people in love. They always behave badly."

Clive called at the house the next morning. Only he knew what a spectrum of torment he had passed through during the night. Rage, bitterness, misery, despair, and at the same time, hope. Had he got it all wrong after all? Was he torturing himself needlessly? They weren't kissing or canoodling or anything, were they? There might be a simple explanation?

Yes, there must be! He would reach the stage of laughing at his own folly. And then the cycle of agony would begin again.

Mrs Gascoyne was delighted to see him.

"I thought you'd deserted me, Clive! You've been keeping my daughter to yourself!"

Cathy held her breath, but he replied sombrely, "I'd like to, Mrs Gascoyne."

"Well, perhaps she would too!"

"Yes, all right, Mum, all right," said Cathy hastily.

66

She actually blushed. Her mother noted this with approval.

"I wish you'd call me mother, and not mum," she chided good-temperedly. "It sounds so much better. Clive always does." Always a-flutter in Clive's presence, she giggled. "I mean he calls *his* mother mother, of course–not me–not yet–"

"Yes, yes," said Cathy, and pushed Clive into the kitchen. "For God's sake," she said, low and urgent, "let's get out, shall we?"

They passed Joe, who was up a ladder working at the plumbing for the bathroom, and walked with some embarrassment to the top of the cliff.

Cliff coughed and said stiffly. "I want to apologize for last night."

"Why, Clive?"

"I was rude."

"Oh, no, a bit abrupt, that's all."

Clive coughed again, hesitated, and said, stammering. "I got it wrong. Awful ass. That chap you were with–know this sounds crazy–thought he might be the chap you–er–"

He could not add, "had fallen in love with", because to him the word "love" was unpronounceable. He faltered, "you'd er, sort of, fallen for . . . Got a bit of a shock, naturally, but realize now . . . made an ass of myself . . ."

"Why did you get a bit of a shock, naturally?"

"Well, I mean to say. It's a bit. Sort of. Well, I mean. Isn't it?"

"If I may say so, you sound rather incoherent."

"I mean, it's a bit unlikely, isn't it? I mean . . . artisan . . . I mean, knowing your upbringing . . ."

"Ah, my type's more someone from a good school, is it?"

"Yes," he said simply.

At which, instead of flying at him in scorn and fury, Cathy felt sorry for him, and guilty. His opinions made her sick. But, truly, there was no malice in Clive. He lacked imagination. But he would never do anyone a bad turn. He would never break a promise. He had real feelings. He loved her. What did that make him, for all his opinions? And in view of the way she was treating him, what could be said for herself, for all her enlightenment?

But in spite of all this, she could not revive any affection for him. Apart from providing alibis, he had become an irrelevancy and a nuisance. His blamelessness made her impatient. Which made her more guilty still. Which made her irritable.

But she kept her head, and said, "We all make mistakes."

"Oh, I know I got it wrong," he said, with relief. Then: "What *were* you doing with that fellow?"

Make a clean breast of it? No. She might as well try to make him appreciate a poem.

"It's—er—to do with my father, Clive . . . It's no secret that we're hard up, is it?—Yes, it is rotten luck. Well, he's terribly worried about the house. The Vicar wants us to leave it. So do the villagers. There's a superstition in the village that if it's occupied, it brings them bad luck—Yes, it is awful rot. But it's getting him down. He's in an awful state . . ."

She gave him a brief outline, speaking of "superstition", but not bothering his head with mention of the selkie or her manifestations.

He said doubtfully, "I don't see how that handyman chap comes into it."

Cathy, too, found that handyman chap an improbable figure in her scenario, but she thought quickly. "I had to tell someone, Clive. He's knocked about the world a bit. I thought he might come up with something."

"Weren't you taking a risk, telling him?"

"Oh no, it's in his interest for us to keep the house on."

"That's true . . . I don't doubt he's sharp. They're like a cartload of monkeys, Cockneys . . ." His face lit up. "And that's all it was? You just wanted to talk to someone?"

". . . yes," said Cathy, feeling dishonoured.

"But you could have told me!"

"Well, I have, haven't I?"

There was something wrong with that, but she was too quick for him. He said, "Yes." He shook his head for a moment, puzzled. But he was much relieved.

Then, as if he were strangling. "I mean . . . there's . . . no one else, is there?"

". . . No . . . no. There's no one else."

Still, I didn't tell him any lies, said Cathy to herself.

I didn't tell him the truth, either.

I told myself he "deserved" it.

But his deserving it came in awfully useful for me, didn't it?

She was not on very good terms with herself. But she could not spend too much time reproaching herself over Clive, because there was Joe's letter to consider. He had worked at it late into the night. It contained no trace of his living self. It was in Business English.

". . . referring to the subject of employment, you may be acquainted with the fact that I have recently entered into business on my own account . . ."

"Very good, Joe," said Cathy. "Very business-like."

"Oh, you reckon?"

"Oh, yes. Very professional. The only thing is, it might be just a teeny bit *too* professional for your dad. He might just think you'd got rather high-and-mighty all of a sudden."

"Patronizing him, like?"

"Well, of course we know you're not, but—"

"Yeah," said Joe, anxiously.

They worked at it apart all afternoon, passing amended versions to each other surreptitiously, like spies with a coded message. At last they produced a letter which satisified them both, or satisfied Cathy, which amounted to the same thing.

9

Mr Gascoyne had taken his pictures for miles around and so far, nobody would buy. After each rejection he became more scathing and disdainful about the art shops. He called them merchant hacks pimping to philistine taste. He called them much more besides, but underneath it all a dreadful doubt was growing as to his own ability, and as to whether he would ever make any more money in all his life.

He was not destitute yet; with the money he had put by he could afford to live frugally for about another three years. But after then, what? He was forty-eight. He was extremely sorry for himself. He said that there was a curse on him. This, of course, brought into prominence what was never out of his mind, the other curse, the one on the house.

Mr Gascoyne went to church sporadically, but he did not really believe what was preached. He avoided thinking about its deeper issues. He wanted life plausible and cosy. Like many people without faith, he was rather superstitious. He touched wood and would not walk under ladders. Deep down, guiltily, he felt that "there might be something in it". And so the legend of the seal girl haunted him, and for all his blustering that it was nonsense he was very frightened.

He had had a wretched day and he could not sleep.

As he lay awake beside his wife, who had walked herself into exhaustion and was dead to the world, he heard singing. It was faint and plaintive, and at first it could be mistaken for the wind, but it drew nearer, and there was no mistaking it, it was singing, a woman singing, and it was so unbearably sad that the gulls flew away out to sea.

Sweating, Mr Gascoyne put on a dressing-gown and crept downstairs.When he gained the kitchen he even picked up a poker, stood wavering, felt ridiculous, and put it down again. He stood in the middle of the kitchen floor, so undecided and so scared that he could not move. The singing stopped.

Mr Gascoyne turned and took a step or two towards the inner door. His clothing unstuck itself from him as he moved. Then he decided that he must prove to himself that he had come down for some purpose, and he made his way tentatively to the window.

A ghastly moon was shining. As if on cue, the figure of the seal girl loomed up from the height of the cliff and began to creep down towards the ruined garden. She had thrown her cloak back fron her throat and her body gleamed with a phosphorescent light. The gleam, of course, was sea salt, and it was fear that was making her move so cautiously, but to Mr Gascoyne she had an unearthly sheen, and she seemed to be approaching with a stealthy and evil intent. His eyes dilated and his mouth went dry.

Fiona reached the kitchen window and pressed her face timidly to the glass. Mr Gascoyne cowered away, thrusting out his hands, his fingers crooked like claws. Then he rushed at the door as if he would smash it down. He dragged the bolt, whimpering to himself. He sent the door crashing open. He cried in a high, cracked voice, "What do you want? What are you doing here?"

Fiona turned and ran. Mr Gascoyne ran a few steps, stopped, and screamed, "How dare you? . . . trespassing . . . private property . . . call the police . . ." Fiona streaked away like a panic-stricken cat and disappeared over the cliff edge, leaving him standing there hot and cold at once, and shaking all over.

Cathy, who was tired out, dreamed that she heard the singing, or rather, supposed herself to be dreaming. Only the commotion below told her that she was awake. And then she was appalled, because she knew that the shrill voice of her father was doing terrible harm. She dragged on her dressing-gown and dashed downstairs, ignoring her mother, who was wavering in her own doorway. Mrs Gascoyne, so brave in some way, was frightened of the dark and all marauders therein. Cathy bore down on her father less like a daughter than a furious mother upon a mischievous child. He was outside the kitchen door, screeching as if to compete with the gulls. He looked so slight and ineffectual that she was sorry for him in spite of herself. She relaxed and said quietly,

"Dad, it's no good yelling like that. Come indoors."

He swung round on her, at cracking point. "What do you mean? The woman was trying to break in!"

"Dad, she's . . . Oh, do come in." She took his arm, but he knocked her hand away so violently that it struck against the doorpost.

"Don't interfere!"

"Dad, please come indoors."

He went in, lit the gas, and crumpled. "Hurt your hand, did you?" he said remorsefully. "I'm sorry."

Her hand was bleeding at the knuckle. "It's all right, it's nothing. Dad, sit down."

He sat down, abject, all dignity lost. Cathy, knowing

73

that the wooing of Fiona had suffered its worst set-back so far, was shaking too, but her concern for him sobered her. She had never seen him in such a state. She placed her damaged hand on his. He looked at it ruefully. With a glance in the direction of the stairs, she said urgently, under her breath, "You know who she is. She's the seal girl. It's no good—"

But he was like a raw nerve that screams at a touch. "Seal girl? *Seal* girl? So what are we supposed to do? Welcome her?"

Cathy drew a breath, exhaled, waited several seconds, and then said quietly, "Yes."

He whipped his hand away from hers and struck it with his fist. "Are you stark staring mad?"

"Listen—"

"Cath, for God's sake! Either she's some demented female tramp or else she's half animal. Are you saying we open our house to a monster?"

"I expect she's house-trained," said Cathy, becoming angry again. She controlled herself. "Please listen—"

She was going to enlarge on her meetings with Fiona. But he broke in.

"Invite her in here? The villagers would lynch us!"

Cathy lost patience. "Rubbish. You know quite well they wouldn't. They'd glare at you a bit harder, that's all. Aren't you supposed to despise them? Don't you call them ignorant peasants? Well, why don't you show them you're superior to them, then? Why don't you—"

"Of all the feverishly muddled-headed—"

"Look. Perhaps she's a tramp. Perhaps she's a monster. All I'm saying is, find out properly. Face her. Then you can have her locked up or something. If you're right, that is. Which as it happens you're not—"

But now her mother, who had been edging down stair by stair, realized that no more than a private

74

quarrel was taking place, and made a dignified entrance.

"What is all the commotion about?"

"A woman was trying to break in."

"What woman?"

"Oh, for God's sake, what do you mean, what woman? *A* woman. A girl. Prowling round here. I shouted at her and she bolted. Cathy, in her infinite wisdom, thinks I should have asked her to be our guest."

Mrs Gascoyne had a tremendous capacity for ignoring whatever she did not want to see. "Take no notice" was her watchword. So, while her husband and Cathy had been involved in the mystery of the house since their arrival, she had held herself aloof from it. But, of course, she was aware that it existed. It was something unmentionable rather than unknown, like sex. Keeping aloof strained her nerves, and being snapped at by her husband nettled her.

"Prowling round?" she said. "I wonder if she has any connection with our labourer friend? Daphne Preston-Browne warned me about that. These people sometimes work in teams. He's had a good look at our silver and things. He could easily leave her some way of getting in."

"Mustn't make accusations," muttered her husband.

Mrs Gascoyne shook her head in a suspicious, knowing way. She was relieved to have found a scapegoat. It averted talk of the supernatural, which was beyond her scope. But then she noticed Cathy's face, white, set, and angrier than she had ever seen it before, and she realized that she had gone too far.

"Catherine, you look so upset," she said. "You're too young and impressionable for this sort of thing. Go back to bed. I'll bring you a hot drink."

75

For answer Cathy sprang up and, flinging open the kitchen door, rushed out into the night.

"Now see what you've done!" cried Mrs Gascoyne. "Get after her! She'll kill herself!"

He called "Cath! *Cath*! CATH-Y!" He scrambled after her, stumbling, catching on bushes, falling. Cathy flung on. She knew this stretch much better than he did. She strode so fast to the edge of the cliff that he thought she must go over it, but she pulled up in time, of course, and stood there, her dressing-gown flapping like a flag, while he hovered a dozen feet behind, eyeing her as if she were a suicide on a window-ledge.

"CATH-Y!"

"Leave me alone."

"Come back!"

"I will when I want to."

But the effect was spoiled by the wind and the seagulls. One cannot repeat heroic speeches to a series of "beg pardons". He looked ridiculous, screwing up his face and cupping his hand to his ear. Cathy took a deep breath and said, "GO AWAY."

He retreated slowly backwards, falling over a few times. Cathy followed, step by step, keeping the distance between them. Outside the back door her mother met her and tried to take her arm.

"Don't come near me," said Cathy.

10

"Did you sleep all right, dear?"

"Yes thank you." Cathy had in fact slept badly, worrying that she had not explained herself at all well to her father, and cross with herself for losing her temper. The trouble with storming through doors is that sooner or later you have to slink back through them.

"Catherine, I'm afraid we all got rather upset last night."

"What's this, the royal 'we'? I think I kept extraordinarily calm, till you started handing out accusations."

"Yes, I'm sorry about that. I know I was rather unfair."

"Oh, well," said Cathy, disarmed, "I'm sorry I flew off the handle."

"Never mind. You do hate injustice, don't you?"

Mrs Gascoyne would make such unexpected observations now and then. She believed, in an unclarified way, that God made Surrey first and the rest of the world afterwards with such materials as were left over, but she thoroughly understood Cathy's moods, and therefore sensed what caused them. For the moment Cathy warmed towards her mother. But the next sentence cooled her again.

"I was not accusing the young man of anything–not at all–"

"But" was the only word that could follow this.

"But?" said Cathy.

"He's a good worker, he's very civil, and he knows his place. But it's only sensible to be on one's guard. Against *any* strange person in one's own house! Now isn't it?"

Cathy nodded resignedly. Alas, that spark of decency had been a flash in the pan. It was the same old mum.

"Besides–I'm surprised you can't see this, really–I don't want to be a snob, but he *is* just a workman, and you can't expect him to have our standards–"

"And he drops his aitches."

"I'm sure I've never said that."

Mrs Gascoyne went quietly about, keeping a cautious eye on her daughter. She would have been surprised to learn what was worrying Cathy more: not the insult to Joe, but the damage that had been done to her chances of befriending Fiona. Cathy herself was taken aback to discover how she felt. Surely she had things in the wrong order? But there it was.

Her father came in.

"Morning," he said. "Storm's over, I hope?"

"Eat your breakfast," said his wife.

He served himself with cornflakes. As he ate, his first breeziness deserted him, and he looked haggard and wretched. Cathy renewed another worry. He was quite ill.

Clive called a little later. She had been afraid he would. He had been confused but not convinced by their last discussion. There was nothing for it but to go out with him for appearances' sake, but she declined to go back to the car, and made him walk out with her at the back of the house, where she could keep an eye on Joe, who was up his ladder working with a blowlamp, and looking annoyingly self-possessed.

Cathy was angry with the world in general. With her parents. With Joe, for his calm. With herself, for throwing herself at him. With Clive, for his mere existence.

Clive was mumbling something all this while in his monotonous voice. She realized that he was asking her a question.

"What?"

Stubbornly, he repeated. "If you just wanted to confide in someone, why go to that workman fellow? Why not confide in me, what?"

"I've told you already."

"No you haven't. You haven't told me why you had to make me pretend to be going out with you when you were actually–"

She could still see Joe, plying his blowlamp.

"I mean, if you just wanted to confide in someone, I don't see why you had to–"

"Oh, Clive, shut up!!"

He reared away, offended. "All right," she said. "I'm sorry, but don't let's go on about it, *please*. Let's go to the village. I've got to buy some things."

"I wanted to go there in the first place," he muttered, aggrieved.

They trooped back to the car in silence. As they went past the house the annoying Joe glanced down, but without a flicker of recognition. Clive looked sullen and was brewing a temper. They drove down into the village.

"Stop here, please."

Cathy went into the chemist's and asked for a brand of lipstick which was in universal supply. Behind the counter stood the village belle, with peroxided hair, plucked eyebrows with half-moons pencilled over them, circles of rouge on her cheeks, and her mouth a scarlet cupid's bow which glistened like jam.

"None left," said the overalled beauty.

"But you've got a caseful on this counter!"

"All on order."

"Do I understand that you refuse to serve me?"

"Understand what you loike."

"Thank you for being so helpful."

There were other shops to visit, but she did not dare go to them for fear of the same treatment. It was her first experience of social ostracism. Fiona must have been shunned like this by the forebears of these same villagers. It was the deadliest of weapons, because you had nothing to fight it with.

"Let's go on to the next village."

Clive started the car, and simultaneously started his protests again.

"I say, look here, Catherine, if you just wanted to tell someone your worries, why did you have to—"

"Clive, stop the car."

"Catherine—"

"Stop, please." She got out. "Thank you. I've had enough. Go home."

"Look here—"

"Good-bye." She slammed the door as if she were throwing the discus, and strode back into the village in a mood to trample anyone who got in her way.

"You're back very early," said her mother.

"Yes."

"Not fallen out with him, have you?"

"No, no."

"Then why are you . . . ?"

Oh, this perpetual need for lying! "His mother wanted the car back early."

"She *would*," said her mother darkly. "She doesn't

approve of you, that woman. Thinks you're not good enough for them."

"I'm content that she should think so."

"Yes, the very idea–!"

Cathy being home, Mrs Gascoyne decided to do some shopping of her own. "Now listen, dear," she said. "I don't want you to stop speaking to our friend round the back. I'd never want you to be uncivil. But he's got his work to do, as I'm sure he'd be the first to agree. And it's always as well, you know, to keep yourself to yourself . . ."

This was worse than raw snobbery, this creepy diplomacy.

"Yes, all right."

"Just be pleasant, and let him do his work."

"Yes, all right."

Cathy sat down at the kitchen table and breathed deeply and regularly until she felt a little calmer. She disliked everyone. Was that true? Well, at any rate, she was jolly well going to know where she stood. Upon which she rose up, marched rather than walked to the back of the house, and stared up at Joe. He gave her his grin, which was a most attractive one, a spontaneous splitting open of cheerfulness, but continued using his blowlamp. It was a roaring, deafening thing. She waited at the foot of the ladder, grimly patient. The blowlamp stopped, allowing her to hear the sound of the waves and the screeching of the gulls. She said, "Joe?"

He looked down, good-naturedly enquiring. Like the head prefect on Sports Day, her voice brittle in the open air, she demanded:

"Do you love me?"

"Blimey," he said, "you asked that straight, didn't you?"

"Well, answer it straight, then. Do you?"

"Yes."

Then Joe said, "Better get on now," and lit his blowlamp again.

Cathy retreated to her bedroom, and, having made sure that Joe couldn't see in, sat on her bed and permitted herself a small, secret smile. She felt cunning, as if she had scored over Joe in some way. She felt as you do when you wink at your self in the mirror over the shoulder of the one who is embracing you.

She was elated, nevertheless, even a trifle light-headed. She lay back on her pillow and watched the motes of dust floating in the shaft of the sun. She was floating, too. Her dingy room was filled with the dancing brightness of sealit air.

And then, to her annoyance, she found that she was crying. It was like finding blood coming from a cut; the tears were involuntary, and not a conscious part of her. She was not, she found, totally elated. There was the merest twinge of dismay. She felt committed, as if she had signed on in the Foreign Legion. Good Heavens, there was no pleasing her.

Her mother came in below.

"Catherine!"

Cathy scrambled up, deploring the fact that there was no water up here to wash her face. She did her best with a licked handkerchief, and hurried downstairs, to find her mother sitting at the kitchen table, looking weary and defeated.

"Things have got to a pretty pass! None of the tradespeople will serve us now!"

"I know, they tell you some tripe about everything being on order."

"That's right, when it's there before your very eyes!

They won't even let me order, either!"

"They really mean to drive us out."

"They won't drive me out so easily. I'm at my best when I'm up against it."

"Yes, you are Mum. Good for you."

"We've got to keep this from your father. He's worried enough as it is."

For the second time that day–probably a record–Cathy positively liked her mother.

"Don't worry. I'll just go to the next village and shop for you there."

"I would be glad . . . It's all to do with this nonsense about the house being unlucky, isn't it? Your father knows more about that than he cares to tell me . . . Of course, I'd be the last person to know, yet if it weren't for me . . ."

Yes, it was ridiculous, everyone being kept in the dark by everyone! It was high time that her mother was let in on a few things. She might be unexpectedly sympathetic. Cathy quite liked her for the moment.

She set herself to deliver. But her mother was watching her face with a different interest.

"Catherine! Have you been crying?"

11

That afternoon Cathy paid a visit to the post office. The whole village was glazed with heat, the high street was empty, and so, to her relief, was the shop itself.

The blue-eyed postmistress retained her smile. Cathy wondered, rudely, if she would still keep it if one went behind the counter and began removing her clothes. But under the smile she wore a guarded look, as if she were ready to throw her body on top of all her goods if Cathy tried to snatch anything.

"All right," said Cathy, "this isn't a raid. I just want your advice. None of the shops in this village will serve us. Why?"

"I reckon you know as well as I do."

"No, no one has explained."

"Well . . . between ourselves, your dad were best advised to leave that house. Better take the cottage."

"Ah, you've heard about the cottage."

"Oh yes, not much goes on in this village that I don't know about."

"So why won't they serve us?"

"You know quite well. It's the seal woman. She comes back when the house is occupied. Some of the fishermen have seen her lately. Swimming. Naked. Their wives are real cross."

"Why, because she's—" Cathy hesitated a second—

"naked?"

"That's right. It's indecent. And they say she's keeping the fish away."

"Then they're superstitious idiots."

"Steady on, now. You don't know everything, just because you come from London."

"Surrey, actually."

"You've seen her yourself," said the postmistress, whose smile had frozen. "Do you say she's a normal woman?"

"No, but–"

"So she's abnormal? So why believe one thing about her and not another? Why call other folk superstitious?"

"Yes, that's very logical," said Cathy, "but consider it from our point of view. My parents feel as if they've been hit over the head without provocation. They bought the house in good faith."

"My, my," said the postmistress, "you're a proper old-fashioned little thing, aren't you? Speak real grown-up, don't you? Well, I'll grant you've been unlucky, but that don't really help matters, and you're still best advised to leave that house. I'll just tell you something, now." She leaned over the counter, looked carefully round, and whispered, *"They're planning to get rid of her."*

"How?" asked Cathy, trembling.

"Now that I don't know. They don't tell me all their secrets, because I'm a stranger here. I know they're posting guards, keeping a lookout for her." She eyed Cathy's shocked face. "Don't go rushing off blaming them, now. Polraddon folk keep themselves to themselves. What they do is their own affair, they reckon. And they'll do it their own way."

"And I'm supposed to think that that's all right?"

"You're on her side, aren't you?" said the postmistress curiously, and not unsympathetically. "Now there's a strange thing. Now: if you'll take my advice, you'll leave strictly alone. You go stirring up trouble, you'll get outsiders interested in her, and you'll know what'll happen then? They'll hunt her without mercy. They'll never leave her alone. They'll make an exhibition of her."

After their last exchange of words, Cathy felt rather shy about the next meeting with Joe, much as one might feel, she supposed, on one's honeymoon night. Now that she had made him agree that he loved her, she didn't want him to demonstrate the fact, not immediately, not yet. He attracted her very much, physically, but all the same she wanted peace, a short while in which to adjust herself to her emotions. The male sex, she feared, would never understand such a state of mind.

The revelation was that Joe did understand. When they met his eyes twinkled for a moment and he then began talking about another topic. He knew about people, Joe. And animals too; all living things. He knew their right to exist untrammelled, to be themselves. Animals accepted him because he accepted them. Not all human beings knew how much they were honoured.

"I've been thinking about your 'selkie'," he said, stressing the word comically. "When I walked up to her on the beach, I didn't show I was nervous, did I?"

"No, cool as a cucumber."

"Yeah. I said that she could smell my fear, didn't I, but since then I've thought, well, I've often been frightened before, who wouldn't be, going up to some blooming great dog snarling at you, but the thing is, you don't want to show your fear, see, you sort of lock it in, and I can do that, not many people can. It's a gift, as you might say. And I reckon I was doing it when I went up to her, just the same."

"So what does this prove, Joe?"

"Well, she wasn't frightened of my fear, she was just frightened of *me*, because I was a man."

"You mean she's been frightened by a man before?"

"Yes. Or men. She's frightened all right. She was frightened by laughter, wasn't she?"

"This is very clever of you, Joe," said Cathy thoughtfully.

"How come?"

Cathy told him about Fiona and the villagers. "The postmistress said they're planning to get rid of her! What do you think that means? They couldn't kill her, could they? It would be murder, wouldn't it? The postmistress said that if I interfered I'd attract the attention of people from outside, who would hunt her as some sort of freak, like the Loch Ness Monster, I suppose." Cathy paused and contemplated a picture of Fiona being made to catch fish or jump through hoops, on show at half a crown a head. "But they couldn't do that, could they? She's a *person*. The Home Office would stop them, wouldn't they?"

"Oh, yes, they'd stop them, and then they'd put her in some bleeding institution."

"Oh, my God, yes," said Cathy. Fiona, the Feral Girl of Polraddon. There would be articles about her in the magazines. "Joe—you are looking for that seal skin, aren't you?"

"Yes, not having any luck, though. I must say, I still find it hard to take, a seal turning into a woman!"

"Oh, Joe, don't you change, you're my only hope. Caterpillars turn into butterflies, don't they?"

"Oh yes, but you know that's not the same. I can't imagine how it would do it. We've got a seal skin in our digs in Marazion, and I look at it, and I think–"

"Seal skin? A real one?"

"Yes. I look at it, and I think–"

"Joe, get it! Borrow it! Bring it to me! Will you?"

"But this can't possibly–"

"No, no, of course it can't be, not Fiona's own skin, but if I could show it to her she would know I understand. She can speak English just a little. Don't you see? It would form a link betwen us! She's so desperately suspicious of us all, but this could help win her round. Don't you see?"

"Ye-es," said Joe. "It depends how you go about it. Don't go flapping at her as if you were offering coloured beads to blooming savages, will you?"

"No, Joe," said Cathy with restraint, "I shall not flap it at her as if I were offering coloured beads to blooming savages."

Joe roared with laughter to hear Cathy's precise accent repeating his words. "You're a girl, you are," he said. "You really want to help this girl, don't you?"

"Joe, you have grasped the point."

"All right, I'll bring you the seal skin, and the best of luck. Go careful, though."

"She's not dangerous."

"No, she's not dangerous, or I wouldn't let you do this."

"Wouldn't you, Joe?" said Cathy, raising her eyebrows. "Do you know, if you really wanted to stop me, I might even let you. So you love me, do you?"

"That's right. What about you?"

"Can you have a doubt?"

"Are you serious, girl? I mean, you'd, like, marry me, would you?"

"Yes."

"You don't sound too sure about it."

"What more can I say?"

"There's something in your voice."

"Oh Joe, stick to bird cries, you're good at them. Don't try reading the thoughts of girls."

"Meaning what?"

"Look, I would like to marry you. But we're jumping fences, aren't we? I think I'd like to marry you. Well, I'm sure I would."

"Blimey, she-loves-me, she loves-me-not. You don't sound at all convinced."

"Never *mind*. You love me, do you?"

"For Pete's sake!"

"Show me, then."

Cathy got home late that evening to find her parents sitting in a sulky silence, even, possibly, a smouldering one, the kind that usually followed a quarrel. Or perhaps it was on her own account? Had Clive called and blundered into giving her away? Nothing was said, but she went to bed feeling uneasy.

She was just about to blow out her candle when there was a tap on the door and her mother came in. Her heart sank.

Her mother closed the door quietly and sat on her bed.

"Cathy, how have you found Dad lately?"

"Er–" Cathy cleared her throat. (Phew!) "Er, well, very jumpy." (How awful, in spite of her concern for her father, to feel such relief that this was the matter!)

"Yes, he is. I think he's near a breakdown. He's behaving quite insanely. He called on the vicar this morning. He said he didn't, but I saw him going into the vicarage when I was traipsing round the village. He must have been discussing that cottage again, although I can't get anything out of him. And what do you think?

He's raised the insurance on this house! He's nearly doubled it!"

"Oh dear," said Cathy, in a tone that spoke volumes.

"I think he's going mad. I found that there was a cheque missing from the cheque book, and I had to nag him all evening to get the truth out of him. I think he's going mad."

Nightmare speculations loomed up in Cathy's mind. It was horribly clear to her why her father had doubled the insurance, and it was undoubtedly clear to her mother too. They had no need to put what they thought into words. In their conversations, words were merely tokens, and often seemingly irrelevant; unconscious spoke to unconscious, and not always amiably. In this matter, however, they were silently united.

"It's not so much that I'm afraid of what he'll do," said her mother. "I can keep my eye on him, as I always have done. But I can't bear seeing him in this state."

"No, Mum."

"Oh, well, don't you worry. It's not your concern. I shouldn't have told you, really; it's not fair to worry you; but I had to talk to someone."

Cathy was registering to herself that one could be a snob with lousy standards and yet a devoted wife and mother, when Mrs Gascoyne remarked:

"Back late this evening?"

"Yes, we went to a café in St Just," said Cathy cautiously.

"You–you get on all right, do you?"

A wave of weariness swept over Cathy. Caution, prevarication, lying–how sick she was of it! But she replied shortly:

"We get on all right."

"You don't sound very enthusiastic."

Cathy became irritable.

"He's an idiot."

"Oh? He is the captain of his—"

"Oh yes, Mum, I know, and he's their best cricketer, too. I don't care what he's captain of. He doesn't understand anything at all."

"Oh, well," said her mother, with surprising tolerance, "never mind that. It's just as well for them not to be too clever. You'll be able to twist him round your little finger."

"I do not want to twist anyone round my little finger. If ever I marry anyone, I'll want a friend and an equal."

Her mother, in the shadows beyond the candlelight, shook her head resignedly, seemed about to speak, gave up, and went out.

And I nearly confided in her, thought Cathy. What a narrow escape!

While Joe and Cathy were in the café in St Just, Clive went for another of his long walks. As usual, he went near Cathy's house, ending up on the same stretch of beach. The usual emotions poured through him. Rage was one. If he saw her with that fellow again, he'd go straight up to him and give him a straight left to the jaw . . . But the prevailing feeling was despondency. He sat down on a rocky boulder whose fuzz of seaweed had dried in the sun, and gazed at the sea. Oh, Catherine, Catherine!

Clive started, and the next moment flushed all over his body. A naked girl waded out of the waves and sat on a rock by the edge. She was deeply bronzed, sleek and shining wet, and her hair hung about her in coils of black treacle. He had never seen a girl in this state before, except in pictures of statues surreptitiously examined in the art books in the school library.

She was half-turned away from him. He ached to go

on looking at her, yet was exceedingly embarrassed lest he should be caught doing so. He rose and strolled with exaggerated nonchalance towards the cliff path, looking up into the air. When he reached the path he crouched behind a bush and looked at her again.

She sat on the rock in the sun for a while, apparently submitting herself to being admired. The light died round her and turned her to a silhouette. She rose, threw on a cloak of some sort, and began walking up the beach towards the cliff. Her movements were seductive and ominous. Clive crouched lower behind his bush. Soon she was hidden by the cliff. Of a sudden he became inexplicably afraid. Normally he would have walked back to the beach and down to the lower cliff road, but now he did not dare to do so, but began climbing the path instead, in the direction of the house. He had taken only a few steps when Fiona, who had scaled the cliff face like a squirrel, appeared in front of him.

Clive gasped. Face to face with beauty unknown on this planet since before the Fall of Man, he was quite unequipped to meet it. He stammered out a few fragments from the stock of his vocabulary.

"I say—look here—what?"

Fiona glistened before him in the twilight, her great eyes staring.

He stammered idiotically, "Afraid . . . mistake . . . don't know you . . ."

Then he turned and ran and ran, down the cliff path, along the beach, up another cliff path farther along. Fiona shrank back, frightened and bewildered by his panic. Then she ran for cover in the sea.

Clive, panting and wild of eye, reached a farther crest of the cliff. Three people barred his way, two men, in their blue jerseys, and a woman. He all but fell into their arms.

"All right, sir. Easy now."

"Sorry," panted Clive. "Must seem–frightful ass–"

"No, you don't. You've seen the seal woman."

"I suppose I have . . . Is that what she is? . . . All I know is . . . there was this girl . . . She was . . ."

He would not say "naked"; there was a lady present. All three nodded knowingly.

"We understand, young man."

The woman said, "Now, she's real, isn't she? Vicar keeps telling us she's superstition. We know better. There's a curse on Polraddon till we're rid of her."

"We be on the lookout for her now," said one of the men.

"But–look here–who–what–*is* she?"

"Seal woman," said the woman. "Witch."

"But–" said Clive. "You mean, she's some sort of vagrant? Well, look here, hadn't we better tell the police?"

"Police'll be no good."

"Then what are you going to do?"

The woman answered. She was about thirty-five, and bonny, but her healthy face was transfigured by a smile so cruel and cunning that it shocked Clive to look at her.

"You know what they do to witches, don't you?" she said.

12

Joe had put up a partition in the large third bedroom, and was turning the one half into a bathroom. This was urgently needed. At present the family used a tin bath, which, although so small that one's knees touched one's chin when one sat in it, held a surprising quantity of water. A kettle was boiled on the antique kitchen stove, and a pail was filled and carried upstairs. Many kettles went to a pail and a disheartening number of pails went to the bath. Cathy was resigned to standing upright and "washing down" in two tepid inches.

Joe had already hauled the new bath into place through a great hole in the outer wall, and was now fitting in the pipes before casing them round with the old stones. Although he had little hope of finding the seal skin, he looked all the time, conscientiously, for any place in the house where it might be hidden, but the house was squarely and simply built: no loft, no hidden nooks or corners, and certainly no secret passages.

He had brought "his" seal skin from his lodgings, as promised, but so far Cathy had not been able to get a look at it. Her mother hovered behind her whenever she went near Joe, and her father, too, wandering fretfully about the house, kept going to watch Joe at work.

"You ought to give it a rest, old man," he said, in his special matey voice.

"I'm all right, sir."

"You work too hard."

"Oh well, there's a lot to do."

"Yes, but you shouldn't overdo it. Why, you work like a beaver, seven days a week! Why don't you take a day off? Say, next Sunday?" Mr Gascoyne was as persistent as a doorstep salesman. "It would do you a world of good."

"Thanks very much, sir, but I want to get on."

"Have a rest, and you'll work all the faster."

But his wife, who had been lurking on the landing, intervened.

"I'm sure Stoneham knows best, dear."

And when she had drawn her reluctant husband out of earshot, she hissed at him: "For Heaven's sake don't encourage him to drag it out! We've got to get the bathroom done, the electricity put in, the kitchen rebuilt—and in my view, the sooner we're done with *him* the better!"

Cathy, quietly eavesdropping on all this, tiptoed into the new bathroom as soon as she dared.

"He wants you out of the way, doesn't he?"

"Yes. He's in a right state, isn't he?"

"Yes, he is, and don't keep saying he doesn't know he's born, and all that, because he's worried and doesn't know what to do. He hasn't made a penny since he lost his job."

"Oh yes," said Joe, "I know how he feels, all right, I've seen it before. And if you don't mind my saying so, he's not going to make any money, not with the pictures he paints. They're O.K., but it's all been done already. There are thousands of pictures like that down here."

"What ought he to paint, then?"

"Girls."

"*Girls*?"

"Yes. Everyone likes to see a girl. You know, girls in boats, girls lying on the beach, girls on the cliffs with the wind blowing them about. He could do that, couldn't he? I should imagine he has quite a feeling for girls."

Cathy's eyes widened; Joe had remarkable intuition. "And you think the art shops would like that sort of thing?"

"I wasn't thinking of the art shops, more the souvenir shops, you know, where they sell piskies and them little china things with messages on them."

"'Elp yersel tu sugar'," said Cathy, shuddering slightly. "And I have to suggest this? He'd go mad."

"Seems to me he's doing that anyway."

"Joe," said Cathy, "you amaze me. But I take your point. I wonder how I'm going to put it to him?"

Later that afternoon she was able to examine the seal skin in comfort. It was in better condition than she had expected; not a rug for the floor, trampled by many feet, but a decorative piece which had been hung over an ottoman, and was little worn. The face and the domed head were formed over some stiffening material, the mouth curved and simpering, and the artificial eyes gazed beguilingly upwards, like those of a waif on the cinema screen. A cuddly, endearing creature. Cathy rubbed her cheek against it and ran her fingers through the silver-grey fur.

"This should do the trick."

"You mind how you go, now."

"There's no danger, Joe. I'll be in much more danger telling my father to paint saucy girls for pisky shops."

She put the skin in her carrier bag and zipped it shut.

*

96

Clive was worried. What the woman had said on the cliff top shocked him. If she had meant what he thought she meant, some nasty mob action was being prepared, and he deplored mob action. He was not made by nature to appreciate the true beauty of Fiona, but he did realize, even from the glimpse he had had of her, that there was no evil in her. His flight had been just a reflex action. He thought that she should be put into care. Clive was a great believer in institutions.

At school he had been taught to use his own initiative. After consideration, therefore, he took himself to the local police headquarters. The police, in his world, were disorder's final solution. In plays, in stories, the way of the transgressor ended with them. "Take him away, officer!" And the culprit was taken away, heaven knew where, to some limbo beyond the pale.

"Polraddon?" said the police sergeant. "Very rare to get trouble from Polraddon." He was a heavy, imperturbable man. "One case of drunk-and-disorderly—if my memory serves me right—let me see—seventeen years ago. Armistice night. Peaceful, is Polraddon."

"There was this girl," said Clive, with some embarrassment. "Came up to me. Absolutely starkers."

"Beg pardon, sir?"

"Running about the beach with no clothes on."

"Really, sir?" The sergeant looked at him with a new eye of interest. "Are you charging her with indecency?"

"No." Clive described his encounter with the fisherfolk, except that he changed his frantic run into a resolute walk. "They said something about 'You know what people do with witches'. Sounded pretty grim."

"Did they now?" said the sergeant thoughtfully.

"Thought you ought to look into it."

"Quite right. So we will."

"That girl needs taking into care, too."

"Yes, sir." There seemed just the slightest hint of mockery in the way he called Clive "sir", but Clive, who was sensitive about his own dignity, might have imagined it. "Mind you, we might have a job catching her, and so might they. From what you say, she's a good swimmer. Still, we'll find out what they're up to, and if it's against the law, we'll put a stop to it. You were right to report it. We'll keep in touch with you."

Cathy lay awake into the small hours, thinking of the sugar-faced seal in her carrier bag, and worrying about Fiona. The postmistress had said, "They're planning something." That was horrible. She must be warned, somehow. The trouble was that Cathy's father, always a light sleeper, was of late sleeping very badly, and would be sure to hear if she tried to go out.

She half-expected Fiona to creep up to the house again. But there was nothing but the crying of the gulls, which must work in shifts over this bay, for they seemed to go on all night. If you timed it to one of those piercing screeches, you could make quite a loud noise and not be heard . . .

At this point the seagulls made one of their periodic visits to the roof of the house itself, and seemed to be attacking it with circular saws.

Cathy slipped out of bed and dressed quickly. She crept downstairs in her tennis shoes, waited for a chorus from the gulls, and undid the bolt on the kitchen door. It whined horribly and jerked free with a crack like a pistol shot. She stepped outside, waited, holding her breath, for any challenge from her parents upstairs, and then picked her way through the gorse to the head of the cliff.

The moon was full, the cliff was spectral in its light,

and the path was chequered with shadows. When she stepped into these chilly patches she could not see her way. She all but lost her nerve several times as she inched down the path. She knew this route well by daylight, but darkness made all the difference. Her carrier bag was a handicap. She tripped once or twice, and having sunk to her knees in fright, had scarcely the courage to get up again.

She clung to a flimsy bit of heather and swayed on her feet. She shouldn't have come. What did she hope to achieve? The odds were she would break her neck. The drop over that edge was sickening. But to go back now would be worse than to go on.

At last she reached the sand. There was about a yard of it to walk on; the tide had just turned. Water oozed up to her shoe-laces.

"I must be mad," said Cathy.

Then she called "Fiona!" Brutally, the wind tore the sound from her lips. She tried again, trying to carry down-wind. It seemed to be blowing in all directions. She drew the name out, almost yodelling it: "Fi-o-ona-a!" Like Mary calling the cattle home, she thought. Like calling the cat.

No response, no one, nothing. Suddenly Cathy was sick with fear. The shore and the sea and the towering cliff were ghastly in the moonlight. The endless, senseless shrieking of the gulls lacerated her nerves. The climb back up the path would be dreadful.

And Fiona. Having come down here to meet Fiona, Cathy had a terror of facing her. Even her beauty was terrible. She was non-human. Cathy did not fear that she might be evil, or even dangerous. She feared her innocence. She feared facing her with her shifty and devious self. She feared her with the fear of shame.

A surge of panic to get off this beach at all costs drove

her to scramble a few yards up the path, head down, peering at her uncertain feet, and when she stopped to recover her breath, and looked up, she saw the seal girl right in front of her.

She clapped the back of her hand to her mouth. The moonlit tableau reeled.

But if she faltered now, Fiona would turn in a flash and take to the sea. She felt her own fear, an urgent current, and she felt Fiona responding to it. And so they hesitated, Cathy weak with the effort of keeping still, and Fiona poised for flight. But Cathy took her hand from her mouth and reached out to the selkie, and slowly, slowly, with infinite trembling caution, Fiona reached out from under her cloak.

Cathy said. "Fiona–can you understand me?"

Fiona smiled and said, "Yes?"

"Fiona–try to understand–you must be on your guard–er–careful–the village people are planning–plotting?–something against you–"

Fiona smiled and said, "Yes?"

It was hopeless. It was like trying to converse with the girls from the Continent who came to school "on exchange"–simplify as you might, your speech was always choked with idioms. Cathy stopped. She said tentatively:

"Fiona?"

Fiona smiled.

"Fiona. I am your friend. Your friend. Your friend."

Fiona understood the word "friend". She reached out and held Cathy's other hand.

"*Ow haradow-vy,*" she murmured.

It is the old Cornish language. It can be translated "my dear", but the sociable English term does not get near it. It is intimate without insinuation and familiar without impudence. It is both sweet and fresh. It is like the murmur of the sea in a shell.

Cathy smiled so ingratiatingly that it almost hurt her. "Well, that's a start, anyway," she said. "Now look–I've got to get through to you, even if it takes till morning. Got to go carefully with you, haven't I? Win your confidence, eh? What was it you said" Cathy had a good ear for languages. "Oo hurruh-doo vee?"

Fiona's great, dark eyes lighted. "*Ow haradow-vy*", she said again. Cathy stepped up beside her and took her arm.

Standing as close to her as this, she understood why Fiona generated fear. It was not exactly fear; it was awe. Until this moment, she had thought of Fiona's extreme nervousness as like that of some reluctant animal who cannot understand human intentions–like a squirrel or wild rabbit which cannot grasp that all one wishes to do is stroke it. She saw now that, to Fiona, she herself was the animal, and that Fiona was cautious with her as she herself would be with some half-tamed creature who might suddenly relapse and bite.

Joe had said, "She's animal, yet she's more than human." Cathy saw now what his intuition had told him. Fiona was one with nature as mankind must have been before death came into the world. She was as superior to Cathy and her kind as she was immeasurably older. If she ran from human beings, it was because no human being was to be trusted. They were perverted and treacherous. It was a humbling discovery. Something of the sort was said in church, of course, but it had never struck home. This was the shock itself.

Cathy said. "You are looking for your skin, aren't you? In our house? Your seal skin?"

Fiona smiled and said, "Yes? I go with you to the house?"

"House" was the key-word; "skin" didn't seem to

101

have registered. "Yes, yes," said Cathy, nodding vigorously. "To the house. Yes. But–we look for your skin, yes? Seal skin?"

And now the triumphant gesture. Cathy unzipped her carrier bag and drew forth the seal skin, with its coy face. "Like this?"

An appalling thing happened. Fiona's eyes blazed, not exactly with terror, but with a kind of rage of disappointment. She recoiled from Cathy as if she were contaminated. Cathy, in all justice without cause, was flooded with a sense of disgrace and shame. She went cold all over and her hair actually lifted on her head.

"Fiona," she stammered, "please–"

But Fiona went over the side of the cliff, down on to the beach, and into the sea.

"Oh, God! What have I done wrong now?"

She sank to her knees, twisting the wretched seal skin in her hands, and stayed so, stunned and humiliated, for fully five minutes. Then she carefully restored the skin to her bag.

"Well," she said. "That didn't work, did it?"

She looked round. It had grown lighter. She could see the sea, leaden in the first greyness of dawn. She began to climb the path. She felt sick with disappointment. What hope was there now?

At the top of the path, by the edge of the cliff, were two fishermen, absorbed in doing nothing, and looking, as their kind always do, as natural a part of the landscape as the rocks.

Cathy had regained her poise. "Good morning," she said, in her clear-cut, too-confident voice.

Their faces were dead serious. One said, "Up early, missie."

"Yes," said Cathy coolly. "So are you, aren't you?"

They had no answer to this. She went back to the house.

102

13

The next day Joe actually asked for a day off. He had no
need to do so, being his own boss, but his anxiety to
please made him over-apologetic. He stood diffidently
in the doorway of the room where Cathy was finishing
a belated breakfast.

"I've had a letter from my dad–my father," he
explained. "He's coming to see us."

"Doesn't he live with your mother, then?" asked Mrs
Gascoyne.

"No, we haven't seen him for over eighteen months."

"Is he a sailor?"

"No, he walked out on us, like, left us, to look for
work."

"I see," said Mrs Gascoyne distastefully. This was the
kind of behaviour you could expect from people of
this class. It was in keeping with putting coals in the
bath. "And has he now found work?"

"Yes, but I want to get him to come in with me. He's a
skilled man."

"Indeed," said Mrs Gascoyne. A new possibility
nettled her. It was that Joe and his father might make
money. "These people" often did make a scandalous lot
of money, which they then probably spent in drink and
betting.

Cathy, hating this interview, was examining her face

in the bowl of her teaspoon, and giving herself a monstrously high forehead by tipping it about. "Tell her to mind her own damn business," she said to herself. But it was not in Joe's nature to squash people, and she knew why.

He was fundamentally gentle; it went with his extraordinary sensitivity to the feelings of animals. You couldn't be hypersensitive and tough at once. "Well, I hope you work it out to your satisfaction," said Mrs Gascoyne. "And now, if you'll excuse us, I think we'd all better get on with our work."

Her husband, all this while, had been quivering like a terrier whining to be taken for a walk.

"Of course you should take a day off, old man. Sunday? O.K? Let's make it Sunday. I'm jolly glad to hear your news. Hope it all goes well. A day off will do you a world of good. So we'll say Sunday."

Joe went off to work in the bathroom, where he could be heard singing, the acoustics somewhat favouring it.

> "Learn to croon,
> If you wanna win your heart's desire;
> Sweet melodies of lurv inspire,
>   Romance;
> Just murmur 'Da-da-*dee*-da-dada-doo,'
>   And when you do,
> She'll answer, 'Da-da-*dee*-da-dada-doo'
>   And nestle closer tew yew . . . "

"That's made him happy," said Mr Gascoyne.

"It seems to have made *you* happy," said his wife.

"Oh, I'm glad for his sake."

"I suppose so. I hope he won't want to bring his father in here and start charging us extra."

Cathy slipped into the bathroom a few minutes later.

"What does your dad think of the idea?"

"He's being cagey. He says it appeals to him, but he'd have to think carefully about giving up a steady job. A steady job, at two pound ten a week!"

"You'll have to go about this very tactfully, Joe. I wish I could talk to him. Said she, having made an utter mess of things in another matter," added Cathy. She returned the seal skin. "You can have this back now."

"Oh, no go, wasn't it?"

"Disastrous. Tell you later."

"You're taking it pretty calmly."

"No use throwing a fit. I did, last night, almost. Got over it now. Joe, did you see how pleased Dad was that you're going away for a day?"

"Yes. Dead keen on it being Sunday, isn't he?"

"Yes. I wish he'd tell us what he's up to."

"Ah, but he doesn't want your mum to know, does he? He's afraid she might stop him."

"Yes." Cathy lapsed into gloom. "I think marriage is awful."

"Oh, not all marriages."

"But you never know how they'll turn out till it's too late."

"You're cheerful today!"

"I'm sorry, Joe. Ignore me."

Mr Gascoyne did not go out with his easel, as he usually did, but hung about, wandering from room to room and doing superfluous small jobs. At last he made them some coffee. Over this he said casually:

"You know, you haven't got round to going to that church at Pendeen! Why not go next Sunday?"

"What a good idea," said his wife.

"Yes, sure! It's supposed to be a beautiful old church. You go, then, both of you. High time you had a break from this place."

"It's the bathroom," said his wife.

"What about it?"

"Half the wall's down. He'll never get finished by then. Anyone could break in. There's that gipsy sort of woman wandering about, isn't there? Have you," demanded Mrs Gascoyne suddenly, "told the police about her?"

"Yes, yes," he lied, testily. "Look, never mind that. I'll stay at home."

"Oh no, there's no earthly reason why you should."

"I don't mind in the *least*." He was frantically anxious to get rid of the pair of them. Cathy recalled similar conversations in the past, when he had been planning to entertain one of his lady friends.

"I don't mind in the very least."

But her mother was like a placid chess-player, effortlessly out-manoeuvring a floundering opponent.

"There's absolutely no need. I'm not so very anxious to go to the church in Pendeen. We'll go the Sunday after, all three of us."

"And leave Stoneham alone in the house?" he cried desperately.

"Ah. All right, we'll go whenever we can."

So, after having used up so much charm on Joe, Mr Gascoyne had failed in his little scheme. Cathy found his frustration positively comic. He reminded her of Clive when he was thwarted of a chance for some necking. But no, it was not a laughing matter. He was hollow-cheeked and there was a small, mad gleam in his eye. Near a breakdown, her mother had said. It made her wary of putting Joe's idea of "drawing girls" to him.

That afternoon Cathy and her mother had to pay a return visit to Mrs Preston-Browne in her holiday cottage near Pendeen. Cathy received this news with ill grace.

"Oh, Mum, must we?"

"I'm afraid we must," said Mrs Gascoyne, almost apologetically. She herself expected to feel like the vanquished queen in some ancient war, being paraded in chains at her enemy's court. "It'll be all right for you, anyway–you can disappear with Clive."

The cottage was near the bus stop just outside Pendeen. It scored a knockout win for Mrs Preston-Browne. Outside it was prehistoric stone; inside chintzy, spick and span, and thoroughly modernized, with wall-lights shaped like candles and electric fires with imitation coals. Its very existence declared that the Preston-Brownes had always been more affluent than the Gascoynes, even in the latter's days of plenty.

Mrs Gascoyne set her face in a martyred smile of admiration and resigned herself to a harrowing afternoon. Conversation, however, was easier than she had expected. Mrs Preston-Brown had news.

"I must tell you. Clive met this Wild Woman at Polraddon. On the beach-near your place. She was-well, you'd better tell them, darling. Discreetly!"

"She was–well, she didn't have a stitch on," said Clive, colouring. "She came right up to me. I ignored her and walked on. I met some local yokels. They had some yarn about a seal girl."

"Good gracious," said Mrs Gascoyne, "that must be that creature my husband found prowling outside our house. Nothing on?–how disgusting! A seal girl? A demented thing who ought to be locked up, I expect."

"Yes, that's what we think," said Mrs Preston-Browne. "There are homes for these people, aren't there?"

"There must be some connection between her and

107

this superstition about our house," said Mrs Gascoyne, very thoughtfully.

"Oh, is there one? You must tell me. Clive's been to the police."

"Have you?" said Cathy.

"Yes, but-"

"When was this, Clive?" said Mrs Gascoyne.

"The night before last."

"But weren't you out with him then?" said Mrs Gascoyne to Cathy.

Cathy felt Nemesis at her shoulder. But Clive stepped in quickly.

"That's right, she was. It was afterwards. I was-I was taking a walk."

"Oh."

Pink in the face, perhaps from describing the Wild Woman, perhaps not, Clive said to Cathy, "Talking of walks, would you care for one now? Lovely view."

"Yes, very much."

They went out, followed by Mrs Gascoyne's approving gaze, and a wry one from Mrs Preston-Browne, who looked as if she were lending something she might not get back.

Cathy said, "Thanks for coming to my rescue!"

"Any time," he said glumly.

"But about the girl-Clive, it wasn't much good going to the police. You see-"

"I did it for the girl's sake."

"Did you, Clive? In what way?"

"I didn't like the attitude of those villagers. They were in a very ugly mood. They were on the lookout for her."

"And you thought she ought to be protected?"

"Yes, I did. They shouldn't take the law into their own hands. That's mob rule. Can't stand for that."

"Well, good for you!"

"Oh, you think so?"

"Yes, you were quite right. It does you credit!"

These were her kindest words since he had come down here. Much encouraged, he tried to put an arm round her. She gently and amicably disengaged herself.

"I'm so glad you felt like that about her, Clive. You're right to take her part. You see, I've seen her too, several times . . ."

Cathy decided that the whole selkie legend would be too much for Clive all at once, but she told him, in strict secrecy, how the girl had saved her from drowning, and how they had tried to talk to each other. She did not mention the visits to the house, or anything that could possibly show the girl in a suspicious light. She spoke of her timidity and apprehension, yet her evident yearning for friendship. She spoke of her phenomenal swimming and her mysterious personal aura, and, of course, of her beauty.

"Didn't you think she was beautiful, Clive? I think she must be the most beautiful thing ever seen on this earth."

Clive said, "Steady on, old girl."

"I beg pardon?"

Clive coughed and turned extremely red. "Cath–I–I can't help feeling you're going too far. I mean, we all know . . . girls at school get crushes on mistresses–and other girls . . . that's all right, of course . . . passing phase . . . all go through it . . . so long as you don't let it get out of hand . . . but, um, can get . . . sort of unhealthy, what?"

Cathy gazed at him, at first, in amazement, but adjusted herself. This was Clive.

"Yes, Clive, I get the message."

"Just thought . . . friendly warning . . ."

"Very friendly. I'm warned." Then: "In an ugly

109

mood, you said? Clive, did they say what they were
going to do?"

"They're hunting for her."

Cathy had a horrible vision of them trawling for
Fiona, and bringing her home in a net.

"One of them, it was a woman, said something about
'you know what they do to witches'."

Cathy closed her eyes.

14

Mr Gascoyne was not getting far with his picture of Polraddon High Street. He could paint nicely, with a feathery, suggestive touch, but he had lost this lately. He kept overpainting, dabbing here and there, so that the picture lost all delicacy, and became hard and bright like enamel on tin. He went on with it because it got him out of the house, and he could sit in the sunshine, pretending to paint, his heart no longer in it.

Cathy came down the hill to join him, looking unusually meek and hesitant. Their last exchange had not been a happy one. The trouble was, she was always rôle-playing with him, and seldom the rôle of daughter. Sometimes she was his mother, sometimes his comrade-in-arms. Sometimes she was a nagging wife. This had been her most recent rôle.

"Dad," she had begun abruptly, "Mum says you've doubled the insurance on the house."

"That's a bit of an exaggeration."

"But what are you up to?"

"I can't talk about it now."

"What has the Vicar told you?"

"I can't talk about it now."

"Do you know what the villagers are going to do?"

"Better ask them."

"Dad, what are you–"

"You're just like your blasted mother," he had shouted, so that she flinched. "Just remember who you're talking to!"

"Dad, I'm worried."

"It's no business of yours."

No, she had not been tactful. Like her blasted mother? So now she stood submissively before him, with an enquiring humble look.

"Hallo," he said. "Forgiven me?"

"Oh, Dad, I'm sorry."

"Yes, you look it," he said. "You have a great feminine gift for looking sorry. You ought to be in advertising. If you could look like that on a poster, you'd have the nation putting its hand in its pocket."

This was quite like his old self, and what was more, it gave her a perfect opening for her proposal that he should draw girls. She sat down, spreading out her skirt, and leaned back on her hand with her shoulder hunched. It was a slight piece of coquetry, but it caught his eye. His glance softened affectionately. This was progress. The sound of a car came from the road below. Cathy looked round, and saw, to her chagrin, a Riley Nine drawing up. Clive got out.

"*Ow!*" she exclaimed, vexed.

"Come, come," said her father teasingly. He was pleased; he didn't like Clive overmuch, being secretly jealous of him. But Clive's face lit up when he saw them together. He strolled up, greeted them, exchanged a few pleasantries, and said to Mr Gascoyne:

"You'll have heard about this seal girl thing, sir?"

He was pleased with himself, as if about to impart good news.

"Well, the police called this morning. Yes, they have got a move on, jolly good. Well, they got a lot out of the local vicar round here. It seems there's a seal girl legend

112

round here. One of the locals married a woman who was really a seal in human shape, apparently. About a hundred years ago. The villagers thought she was bad medicine. So they got up a thing to drive her away. They rigged up the dummy of a seal, and the dummy of a woman–sounds a bit like Guy Fawkes–tied them together, and burnt them on your stretch of beach–"

Cathy gave a little moan, but he did not notice.

"Seems to have done the trick. She got frightfully annoyed and rushed into the sea and swam away and wasn't seen for ages. Well, now it seems that the villagers believe that this nude female who charges about the beach is the seal woman come back. So they're going to do the same thing again–burn an effigy of her. Of course, there's nothing illegal about a bonfire, so the police can't do anything, and actually, if it relieves their feelings, it's a good thing. It relieves me, actually, because I thought they wanted to burn the woman herself, and I wasn't going to stand for that. Of course, they're an ignorant lot–you know what I think?–I think she's some crackpot who *thinks* she's the seal woman–there are loonies who think they're Napoleon, aren't there?–but if it'll settle their minds, let them have their bonfire–no harm will be done–."

"No *harm*? You think there's no harm in holding a filthy orgy and baiting this girl until she's driven into the sea? So it's a good thing if it relieves their feelings? What about her feelings? She can be destroyed if the rest walk off happy?"

Her father was not listening. He shouted wildly in unison with her. "It's the only way–stop all this hostility to us–can't you *see*–someone's got to pay–"

These last words broke Cathy's control. She gave way to frantic sobbing. Clive tried to put his arm round her. She dashed it away. Her distress was so great that her father was silenced and Clive, who had thought he was on the way back into her favour, was nonplussed. She sat panting and dabbing at her face, recovered herself, and turned on Clive with quiet intensity.

"You're stupid," she told him. "That's what's the matter with you. You don't understand anything. You're stupid, stupid."

Clive, with nothing left to lose, sprang up angrily.

"I'll talk to you when you've come to your senses."

He strode off down the hill and got into his car. She saw the door slammed and heard, fractionally later, the bang. He reversed in a flurry of dust, slewed the car round, and roared off.

Her father, weak and ashamed now, clutched at the chance of changing the subject.

"He's gone off with a flea in his ear! Don't worry, he'll be back."

"I don't doubt it," said Cathy contemptuously. She looked into her father's face, checked a scathing comment on himself, reached and gripped his arm blindly for a moment, and went back up the hill.

"Undignified—waste of energy—useless," said Cathy to herself, and lay back on her bed and tried to sort things out.

Clive's tale had helped her to understand Fiona's suffering, and her fears. She saw now why she had run from the laughter on the wireless, and why the sight of the made-up seal skin had upset her so much. Both were reminders of that evening, over a century ago, when she had fled from the most detestable noise on earth, the derision of a mob.

But what could Cathy do to help her? All she had done so far had only made matters worse. Fiona probably distrusted her now above all others.

Indeed, by befriending her at all, she was putting her in danger. To be truthful, the local vicar was right; they should leave the house, because while they stayed there, Fiona could not resist coming to the house. She would be safer out at sea.

Yes, but still lonely and lost and unfulfilled. As for her finding her own skin, what chance was there of that?

"I'd say I'm licked," said Cathy to herself. "The villagers are going to beat me to it."

And so, once again, all Fiona was going to get from human beings was hate, or repugnance, rather, the sort of feeling that Cathy herself had about spiders.

Which reminded her of Joe.

"There are good people, Fiona," she declared to the ceiling. "Not everyone's disgusting."

John Tregarthen had loved her?

Joe had been right about him, too. Any fool can love a pretty girl. Fiona needed to know there was something else.

Cathy avoided her father for the rest of that day, and for the next morning too. Not that this was difficult, for he was constantly on the move, making innumerable nervous visits to the lavatory, and frequently going to the cliff top to scan the beach below.

Cathy scanned it too, discreetly, and so no doubt did the appointed vigilantes of Polraddon, but there was no sign of Fiona, day or night. That incident of the skin had scared her off. But Cathy was as sure as were the villagers themselves that she would come back before long, irresistibly drawn to the house. Waiting for her return, and for the villagers to act, was a fearful strain, like waiting for a bomb to go off.

Mr Gascoyne kept up his restless prowling until his

wife challenged him on it. He said that he was thinking of doing "a seascape".

"I hope you'll soon settle down and do it, then," she replied. "You're like a cat on hot bricks."

He became sorry for himself. "Not much encouragement to settle down to anything when everything I do is rejected."

Now was the moment, Cathy decided. "Perhaps you should paint something different," she said.

"Such as what?"

"Well, perhaps you should put people into your pictures."

"Fishermen, you mean?"

"I was thinking, more like girls. Plenty of great artists have painted girls, haven't they? I mean, there's–" For the moment Cathy could not recall a single one.

"Botticelli?"

"Yes! I'd be a free model for you."

"Portraits, you mean?"

"No, more like . . ." Her hopeless ignorance was the drawback here. "'The Boyhood of Raleigh'," she said, helplesly.

"The sort of picture that tells a story," put in her mother, who was taking a great interest in all this.

"Yes, exactly!"

"You did a very pretty one of the Grapefruit Girl, sucking a straw," said Mrs Gascoyne.

"Oh, *that!*"

"I thought it was lovely."

"She doesn't have to be advertising something. I mean, a serious picture. You see, Dad," said Cathy glibly, "your pictures of fishing boats and so on are O.K., but that's all been done already."

"Well, I don't know . . ." muttered Mr Gascoyne, brooding.

116

At least he had not stormed out in a rage. Cathy began working on him, backed up by her mother, who was of doubtful worth, however, because she kept irritating him by reminding him of his advertisement pictures, so that Cathy was hard put to keep the conversation in the right direction. At last, making out that he was only doing it to humour her, he agreed to "knock just one off", and went with Cathy to the top of the cliff, and began drawing her in the sultry afternoon heat.

He did not use oils this time, which were not really his medium, but sketched in pencil, to be water-coloured afterwards, like the illustrations he had once done for the magazines. He used Cathy only as an outline. In this he was lucky, as Cathy's outline was excellent. Once he had achieved it he forsook her outdoor charm for an idealized girl of his own imagining, wide-eyed and wistful, with slightly parted lips. She was gazing yearningly out to sea. The picture was politely erotic, her dress being discreetly unbuttoned and rumpled. He called it "No Sail In Sight". He took it back to the house, coloured it, and painted it over with fixative varnish. The whole thing had taken him about an hour. It was good bad art, slick and competent. He had not spent thirty years in an advertising agency for nothing.

"I think it's lovely," said his wife. "I knew you had it in you."

He put a light frame round it. "All it needs now is a bit of glass," he said.

"They'd do that for you at Sandalls the chemists," said Cathy. "They sell pictures, too."

Yes, Sandalls, who had branches in every big town, went in for art: snarling tigers, elephants crashing through undergrowth, touchingly tearful children, and young girls in their night attire kneeling in prayer.

"M'm," said Mr Gascoyne thoughtfully.

"Oh well," said Cathy to herself, "at least it's passed the time for him."

Mr Gascoyne took his picture to the Sandalls in Truro the following morning, and the manager in charge bought it, not on a commission basis, but outright, giving him a cheque for seven pounds. It would sell, he said, for ten or twelve. If it sold quickly he would take further pictures of the same kind, and if they continued to sell he would consider asking head office to have prints made of them, for sale throughout the branches.

Struggling artists are wont to be extravagantly elated by the smallest success, and Mr Gascoyne returned home almost hilarious with exultation. Smiles broke out like flags on the family faces.

"What did I tell you?" said his wife. "I knew you could do it."

"Only seven quid," he smiled, deprecatingly.

"But it's a start!"

She had her good points, thought Cathy. She loved him as much as Joe's mother loved her defecting husband. She was loyal.

"Well, Cathy," said Mrs Gascoyne, "that was a very good idea of yours, wasn't it?"

Cathy could not resist saying, "I got it from something I heard Mr Stoneham say, actually."

"Oh, good gracious," said her mother, "that was quite accidental, I'm sure. What would such a person know about art?"

15

The next day, Sunday, it rained. It came down in a hissing, leaping, roaring wall, slackening only to a steady downpour. It washed out any chance of the villagers' bonfire. Cathy sat in her room writing belated letters, giving comic descriptions of her new home, and wondering what life would be like here in a hard winter.

Meanwhile her parents, also trapped by the rain, held an endless conversation below. Cathy could hear her mother's cool voice, scarcely ceasing, and occasional rejoinders in her father's cultured tones. She listened at the door from time to time to try to catch what they were saying. She heard Clive mentioned once or twice, but she could not grasp the thread of it.

When she went downstairs it was to find them both curiously tranquil and somehow conspiratorial, as if they were smiling to each other behind her back. It puzzled her. Perhaps this mood had been caused by the sale of her father's picture.

Clive came back, as her father had said he would. He came back in the rain that afternoon. Cathy was in her bedroom again. She opened her door a crack and eavesdropped on the exchange below.

"Is Cathy in, Mrs Gascoyne?"

"Catherine may be in her room."

Clive might well be getting drenched, as this house had no porch, but Mrs Gascoyne did not invite him in.

"Oh. Could I, I mean, see her?"

"Yes, I expect you may, if she's not otherwise engaged."

Oh, Mum! thought Cathy. Engaged in doing what, in this dump on a rainy Sunday?

But she understood her mother. That seven pound sale had restored her morale. Before it, Mrs Gascoyne had suffered a humiliating loss of face; for all her brave pretences, her friends, and Mrs Preston-Browne in particular, had known quite well that her husband was out of work and that they were worried and resourceless. But now Mr Gascoyne had justified himself as an Artist. His picture was on display in Truro. There was scope for superb development of this fact, some of it with a grain of truth in it. "Yes, Sandalls are very taken with his work and they're going to run off prints of his pictures and sell them throughout the country!" Fame, and the hint of an income whose size no one could verify! It did not matter that the income so far was so small. Face was what mattered.

So it was that Mrs Gascoyne was no longer ingratiating to Clive, but condescending and a little distant, and meanwhile the poor lad stood out in the rain. How were the mighty fallen.

"You'd better wait."

Cathy flew back to her writing desk.

"It's Clive."

"Oh, all right," said Cathy, rising.

"No, wait," said her mother, pressing her down. "No need to go rushing down at once. Just let him wait for you a bit. I don't like the way he patronizes you. His mother is to blame, of course. She's brought him up to think he's the lord of creation . . ."

Sorry for him, Cathy greeted him pleasantly enough, and they went off together under his umbrella to his car. In the car, Cathy confined herself to being polite and brief, and they drove to a nearby town to sit on the streaming esplanade, and watch the rain falling from the height of the sky into the sea.

"*Cath* . . ." said Clive, in a low, reproachful tone, and put his arm round her shoulders.

"No, don't, Clive."

He turned away in despair.

"It seems your whole family's turned against me. Your mother went all weird and distant just now. I can't make out what I'm supposed to have done."

She said deprecatingly, "Oh, you've done nothing wrong."

"I have, you know. It's something to do with that seal woman. Can't think what."

Cathy was staring into the rain, at a loss to explain this vagary of fate, when he added:

"The police called this morning about her, by the way. It's decent of them, the way they keep in touch. Or maybe they think I might know more than I've told them. Anyway, it seems that the villagers were planning their bonfire for this evening–"

"This *evening*!"

"Yes, low tide. I say, does that shake you? I shouldn't worry–they can't possibly go ahead if it rains like this."

Oh, please God, let it go on raining!

"This evening," repeated Cathy, dully.

"Yes, weather permitting. I say, Cath, are you all right?"

"Of course I'm all right."

"You look a bit shaken. Don't worry, it's bound to be rained off."

"But it's bound to happen soon."

"Well, honestly, Cath," said Clive, in confidential, reasoning tones, "it would be just as well if they got it over and done with. The police can't stop them, because they're not doing anything illegal. They suggested that I should go along to watch, actually—"

He broke off. As soon as he had spoken he realized he had put his foot in it.

"Who did?"

"Er—the police."

"What for?"

Clive had no skill to talk himself out of this. "Well—for a bit of fun, I suppose—"

Cathy really should have seen that he meant no harm. She should have had more patience with him; but she was too angry for such sympathetic niceties. She sprang to her feet.

"Fun!! Great fun!! Did they sell you a ticket for it? What a pity there are no public hangings these days! You could really enjoy yourself!"

She strode off into the rain.

"Cath!" He bounded after her. "You'll be soaked!"

"Good."

"Come into the car, won't you?"

"Keep your blasted car."

Clive realized that he looked silly, running after her with his umbrella like a butterfly net. Some elderly couples in the other shelter bays turned lack-lustre eyes on him. He went back to where he had been sitting, lowered his umbrella, and slumped down.

"Oh, *Lord*!" he groaned.

"You got rid of him pretty quickly," said Cathy's mother doubtfully. She noticed her daughter's wetness. "Didn't he drive you home?"

"I caught the bus."

122

"M'm. Best not to be *too* high-handed, dear . . . Still, just as well to show him you can be independent . . . "

Cathy dried her hair, changed her stockings, and reflected on this. She was sorry she had lost her temper, not so much for Clive's sake as for her own. She had been losing it too often of late.

16

Cathy sought out Joe, who was outside repairing the bathroom wall. On each descent of his ladder he supplied a section of narrative.

"My old man nearly drove me mad yesterday. No, not quarrelsome or anything, quite the opposite. Tramping around and sleeping in doss-houses has knocked the stuffing out of him. He looks ten years older, and his nerve's gone. All he would say was, 'Got to be careful about giving up a steady job, though, son.' A steady job, when they can sack him any moment! I said, look, Dad. I've got several big jobs lined up that I can't take on yet. I shall lose them, because people will get tired of waiting. (Your vicar's one of them, by the way. He wants his church hall doing up.) I said, look, you can earn four quid a week for yourself, easy, for weeks ahead. Oh, but what about the winter? I said, we'll be busier still in the winter, we're plumbers aren't we, people's pipes go in the winter. 'Got to be very sure before you give up a steady job, though, son.' He wanted my mum to go and live with him in two rented rooms in New Cross!"

"What did your mother say?"

"Didn't know what to say, poor old dear. 'Joe's doing very well for himself, though, Fred.' 'Your dad don't want to take risks, though, Joe.' And then of course he'd say for the fiftieth time, 'That's it, you see, Joe, don't want to give up a steady . . . '–Oh, God give me strength!"

"And did He? I mean, you didn't lose your temper with your father?"

"No. It never does any good. Patient as a saint, I was. Well, a saint who goes in for swearing a bit."

"And did it work?"

"Yes," said Joe, with a tired sigh. "It worked. He's joining me. He's starting work on the vicar's church hall today."

"Oh, good for you, Joe. How did you win him round?"

"I said I'd have to take on an assistant from somewhere, probably some kid just out of school. That got him, because he's still got pride in his craft, he doesn't like to think of a job being mucked up. Yes, he's joined me, and I can tell you, he'll do the church hall proud . . . By the way, is your dad still thinking about buying that cottage? Because, when I took my father to meet the vicar this morning, I thought I saw your dad coming out."

"I was still in bed," said Cathy, vexedly. "Buying the cottage? No, he couldn't possibly. Calling on the vicar . . . What on earth is he up to now?"

Joe had put the bath in and now, on the other side of the partition, was installing a lavatory pan and cistern. It was the first time he had been called on to do this job, and to make sure he had the hang of it he kept walking out to the lavatory in the garden, to study its plumbing. The water-cistern was surely a later addition. Originally, this minute building would have housed a simple earth latrine. It really was a Stone Age structure, cruder than the house, with abnormally thick walls.

Well, it had withstood wind and weather.

Cathy, meanwhile, "sat" for her father once more. This time he was drawing a wind-blown maiden at the wheel of a boat. He was going to call it "Youth at the Helm". He was marvellously relaxed, and she wondered what sedative could be responsible for it. The sale of the picture? Not altogether. There was something else, and she was beginning to feel alarmed. So, when he had made his sketch of her, she left him and went to her mother.

"Mum, what's happened to Dad?"

After a few deliberate misunderstandings and repetitions her mother replied, as if finally confessing:

"Oh, I've managed to talk some sense into him."

"Yes, I see you have, but how?"

"He's like a child in some ways."

"Yes, Mum, we know that. But what have you said to him?"

"He wanted to get us all out of the house, didn't he?"

"Yes, yes."

Mrs Gascoyne looked at her sightlessly, and said in a far-off voice, as if she were recalling some distant memory: "He wanted to burn the house down."

"Yes," said Cathy, with a great patient sigh. She had known this all along, of course. It had been obvious. His craving to get them out of the house, his feverish interest in the villagers' fire—of course, of course: a spark from it, blown from their roof, could be blamed . . .

He was desperate to leave their doomed house.

Obvious, too, why he had doubled the insurance. Yet it was pathetic. Any insurance investigator would discount his "spark from the bonfire" explanation in a few minutes. Besides, the house would not burn. The walls were stone, and the wood was so hard and thick

126

that it would just smoulder. This fact, for some reason, touched Cathy's heart.

Her mother was watching her expression.

"Don't take it so tragically, dear."

"I should have thought it had its serious side," said Cathy, with a smile.

"He'd never have tried it, really."

"No, he wouldn't, knowing him."

"Of course, he always keeps you worried. When he was younger he often threatened to kill himself. When we were first married, before you were thought of. That's something you didn't know, isn't it? It used to terrify me. I was young and inexperienced in those days, and he would go to such lengths–almost to the point of carrying it out. He'd arrange cushions in the gas oven and lie down with his head inside for me to find him. Only he never got so far as turning the gas on. So after a while I realized he never would. And he'd never have tried burning the house down. There's no harm in him, really. He needs play-acting."

"You've really looked after him, haven't you?"

"Someone's got to."

Mrs Gascoyne was thin, with a slightly corrugated neck, and a way of holding her head back, as if offended by the smell of common humanity. It was a supercilious face. But perhaps all this was her only means of defence. She had had her battles.

"All right, Mum," said Cathy. "What did you say to him? I couldn't get near him."

"Oh well, I've known him longer than you."

"Yes. But–"

"Oh, I just talked him round, you know, I can't remember what I said exactly."

Which was not at all satisfactory; but Cathy knew she was not going to get nearer to an answer than this.

She said:

"You've kept awfully calm through it all."

"I did what I always do, I prayed to God, and I hoped my prayers would be answered."

Her mother must set God a problem, thought Cathy. Like Him, she moved in a mysterious way.

She was awakened in an angry and unusually noisy dawn, in which the crying of the gulls was augmented by a confused uproar of another kind.

She was still stupid with sleep. It was an exceptionally angry sunrise, flexing red and yellow at her window.

Sunrise? No, those were flames, and the noise from the beach was human. The bonfire had been started. The villagers had been cunning. They had lit it when there would be least interference.

She lurched from her bed, rather faint from shock, and dragged slacks and a jumper over her pyjamas. Even through her window, insistent through the rest of the noise, she heard the voracious crackle of the flames.

Her father and mother were already up, fully dressed, waiting for her, it seemed. She looked accusingly from one to the other. They took an arm a-piece, comforting her as they used to in thunderstorms when she was little.

"It's all right. There's no harm. No one's going to be hurt."

"Who says so?" demanded Cathy furiously, shaking off their hands.

"This is a village thing," said her father. "It's no concern of ours."

She flung away from them and hurried out of the house. Choosing their steps carefully, they followed her.

128

When she stood clear of the screen of the cliff edge, the fire burst upon her like an explosion. It was enormous, six times the height of a man. It was well away from the cliffs, near the group of rocks where Cathy had first seen the selkie. It was built of old chairs and tables and linoleum and miscellaneous rubbish, and at its peak, barely recognisable but not yet quite consumed, were the two effigies, seal and woman.

It was thunderously ablaze, much too far advanced for any sort of intervention. The villagers, small black figures, stood in a semi-circle, well back from the heat. They were perfectly orderly, like a crowd round a public bonfire on Guy Fawkes Night. They were well pleased with themselves. She could imagine them eating sandwiches. The fire roared to Heaven.

Her parents caught up with her.

Her mother said "Well, now perhaps they'll be satisfied."

Her father said, "You see—there was nothing to worry about, after all." Cathy turned a white, set face on him. "Oh, come on, Cath. Sticks and stones may hurt her bones, eh?—but not a thing like this—"

"You knew about it, didn't you?" she said in a low voice.

"I expect everyone did," he replied easily. "It's been common knowledge."

She turned away. "Come away, for God's sake."

She began to go back, and they followed her, uncertainly. The reflections of the fire lunged and fanned about the house. Into the flickering and flashing light a figure dashed suddenly.

Cathy screamed, "Fiona!"

She rushed towards her, but the selkie was frantic with terror. She made a wild dash past them to disappear over the cliff top. They stumbled back to watch her. Mere seconds later she appeared on the beach, tore past the crowd, and plunged into the sea.

A long "O-o-oh!" rose from the villagers. The clung to one another, frightened and thrilled, as once crowds must have been when they saw a witch consumed by the flames.

17

"Don't want your breakfast, Cath?" said her father.

She shook her head.

He came round the table and put his arm round her.

"Don't be so upset, darling. It's all for the best."

"In the best of all possible worlds," said Cathy, disengaging herself with a writhe of her shoulders.

"Come along, now."

He was so pleased by the banishment of Fiona. It was like the timely death of a tiresome relation, another piece of the general good luck that seemed to be coming their way. Everything was working out fine. There was going to be a happy ending. Mrs Gascoyne had said her prayers, she had given God her shopping list, and He had obliged.

But Cathy felt like a party to something disgraceful, the main party, the criminal. She had failed Fiona, as everyone had always failed her, through one or another miserable failing of their own.

Too dejected to dispute the matter with her parents, she trudged down to the post office for the mail. One or two villagers said good morning to her. This was something new. They seemed ready to chat with her, too, but she nodded briefly and went on.

"No letters for you today, moy lover," said the postmistress. "But you'll find the postman will be calling on you from now on."

"He's had a change of heart, has he?"

"You'll find they'll all be nicer to you from now on."

"How kind of them."

"Oh, Polraddon folk are friendly enough," said the postmistress. "Truth to tell, a lot of them have been sorry for you all along. They know it's not been your fault. And now that you've been so cooperative, they've come round."

"How have we been cooperative?"

"Well, it was your dad, wasn't it? After your young man went to the police, they all felt very uneasy, because although the police couldn't do nothing, they didn't want them to be in on it. They like to keep their movements private, do Polraddon folk. They were afraid you lot would call the police whenever they held their fire. And then your dad tipped the wink to the vicar . . . But you know, don't you?"

"My father promised that if they had their fire in the middle of the night, he'd keep quiet?"

"Why, yes. The police did get to know, of course, but they turned up only in time to see some ashes."

"Well, I didn't know anything about it."

"Really? Fancy. You saw the fire, though?"

"One could hardly ignore it."

"No, a great big blaze, wasn't it?" said the postmistress cheerfully. "Did you see her dash ino the sea?"

"Yes, I did."

"So what about superstition now?"

"What indeed."

"Oh, Cornish people are wise in ways you London folk don't dream of."

"How nice for them that it's all turned out so well."

"It's upset you a bit, hasn't it?" said the postmistress. "Now don't you worry. "Tis all for the best."

Satisfaction all round, mused Cathy, as she went back home. Cost: one tormented innocent. A good bargain.

"Did you hear what my father did?" Cathy asked Joe.

"Well, yes. The caretaker at the church hall told my dad about it. Look, I know how you feel, but you've got to tell yourself, it would have happened anyway, and it's certainly no fault of yours. Don't blame your dad, now. He's been a very worried man. Worried people do awful things. I should know. Ah, come on, girl. I know how you feel, but—"

"You know how everyone feels, Joe. You're unique. But you're wrong about one thing. It *is* my fault."

Cathy would not be consoled. She went to her room and lay staring at the ceiling in a wan reverie, while the racket of Joe's working shook her wall.

It was the worst day of her life. And yet, at the very heart of her despair, there was the weak hope that Joe might yet find the seal skin. A persistent nature, was Cathy's. At last she left her room and ventured into the bathroom, where Joe was fitting the lavatory pan.

He shook his head, anticipating her question.

"It's impossible, isn't it, Joe?"

"Where am I supposed to look?"

It was hopeless, unless they removed the plaster from every ceiling and the boards from every floor.

"Perhaps if I showed her the real skin, she might be frightened again, anyway," said Cathy.

"No," said Joe.

"No," said Cathy. "So we keep on looking."

"You don't give up easily, do you?"

"It's given me up," said Cathy wearily. "Fiona has, too. After last night she might not come back for years. This iron-jawed determination is all very well, but there comes a time when you know you're beaten."

"Don't contradict yourself now, mate," said Joe. "It

hasn't come for you yet."

She laughed resignedly. "I suppose not."

Joe stood back and contemplated the piping.

"I'm just going down to that lavatory in the garden."

"Don't let me stop you."

"No, I want to see how the pipes are fixed."

When he came back, some minutes later, Cathy was still hunched up on a chair in the corner.

"Did you find out what you wanted?" she asked listlessly.

"Yes," he said, with an anxious glance at her, and went on talking for the sake of it. "It's a funny place, that, there are two back walls, one behind the other. For strength, maybe, but the house isn't built like that. I thought the pipes must be between the two walls, but they aren't, they're just run up on the outside of the inside wall, if you take my meaning."

"Two back walls?" said Cathy. "How interesting. Perhaps they just wanted to use up the stones."

Then she stood up.

"Or else . . . "

Joe went out into the garden yet again, and in a few minutes Cathy joined him. She had never really looked properly at the outside lavatory, only at its entrance and interior. The back of it nested in a mass of vegetation, gorse bushes, waist-high grass, convolvulus, and a gnarled tree like an arthritic hand, which twisted into the very structure of the wall. Using a pair of pliers as secateurs, Joe chopped back the gorse bush and ripped up grass and convolvulus with his hands. The tree had so penetrated the outer wall that some of the stones were resting in its branches rather than on each other, and could be lifted out quite easily. He took up a round steel chisel and a heavy hammer and began knocking

134

the cement out between the other stones. Cathy stood so near that the dust settled all over her. Joe removed stone after stone. It was still easy enough; in fact, there was a space between them.

Joe, who had been working patiently but without heart, now glanced at Cathy with renewed interest, and attacked the cement again with such vigour that she recoiled choking from the fresh cloud of dust. Half the wall was opened up now, and the remaining stones leaned groggily in, threatening an avalanche. He took his torch and examined the hole, while various sinister insects scattered to left and right.

About a foot above the ground, propped up by stones at either end, was a narrow board. On it was something folded in a neat square. He drew it out and handed it to Cathy. It was very heavy, for the outer wrappings were seaman's oilskins, layer on tarry layer of them, fastened with tapes of the same material.

They cut the tapes. The oilskin resisted when they unfolded it, as if they were opening a tin. Sheltering behind the outhouse from any view from the house, they laid it on the ground and prised each layer away, until it was all spread open like a ravaged seaweed, and in the centre of it lay what they were looking for.

Cathy lifted it out and unfolded it with shaking fingers. But there was no need for excessive care. It was golden brown and strong, and as soft and supple as if it had just been taken from the seal's body.

"It was worse than killing her, in a way," said Cathy. "John Tregarthen took away her real existence."

"Like I said, people in love behave badly, as a rule. It makes them selfish."

"I wonder what hope there is now."

"Well, this is quite a find, isn't it? I can't get over it.

It's a miracle."

"Yes, but we may have found it too late."

"It's not like you to talk like that," said Joe. He looked at her closely. "Take it easy, now. You're shaking to bits."

Cathy made sure that her parents were firmly based downstairs, and drew the seal skin from the recesses of her wardrobe. She trembled with wonder as she unfolded it, because she was touching magic. It was silky. It was alive. It was a hundred and twenty years old. No: it had lain hidden that time, but in actual fact it was thousands of years old: it was timeless.

She crushed it to her, rubbing her cheek against it. She felt sure that if only Fiona could see it, there would be no danger of her running away again. This was real. That fraud from Joe's lodgings had smelt of man.

She folded it again and pushed it into her large carrier bag. She called good-bye to her parents and left the house. Clive, although this time he did not know it, was providing her with another alibi.

She scanned the cliffs as she went. There was no one in sight. All day, the villagers had been returning to the site of the fire, to gawp idiotically at its remains, and the police had also made a visit, but now the tide was in. There was nothing to look at but water, and when that receded, all shameful remains would be washed away.

She reached her old spot on the cliff path. She looked down at the darkening water.

"Fiona," she called timidly, against the screeching of the wheeling gulls. "Fiona." It was a token call only; she could hardly hear herself.

At this moment, perversely, Cathy even hoped that the selkie would not appear. Then she would be able to go back to her own family, and the village where they were now well thought of, with a clear conscience, in the knowledge that she had tried. She spoke again, more firmly, and again, and again, waiting each time like an auctioneer who knows there will be no more bidding.

"Fiona . . . Fiona . . . Fiona . . ."

"All right, I'll just have to give up . . ."

She turned back, and as she did so the memory of Fiona's terrified dash past the villagers' fire leapt up in accusation. If she gave up now she would never be on good terms with herself again. She faced the sea and shouted angrily to the empty air.

"Fiona, help me!"

Something dark moved across the water a full hundred yards out.

Cathy felt in her bag for the seal skin. She thought of waving it aloft, but dared not. She thrust the bag under the gorse bush and stared again into the dying light. And now she saw Fiona beyond doubt, bobbing at waist height, still no nearer the cliff. She waved and beckoned.

All she wanted was for Fiona to swim in and see the skin. Nothing could be easier, nor harder, because Fiona had all but lost faith in human dealings. She kept far out. She was very wary indeed. Only a pathetic tremor of indecision was holding her there at all. A wrong move, a wrong word from Cathy now, and it would be disaster.

Cathy looked down at the lazily crinkling water.

"Oh, *no*," she whispered.

Ever since she had nearly drowned she had had a fear of water. She was no match for these currents, and if she were fool enough to risk them there was no guarantee that she would be rescued again. She had neither costume nor towel. It was cold.

137

On the other hand, she reasoned falteringly, there was probably less danger now than that other time. Then, the tide had been going out, with tremendous drag. Now, at high tide, the water had just reached that point of balance between flow and ebb when motion would be at a minimum. If Fiona would remain still, it should be possible to swim out to her, and then, if she still wouldn't budge, to swim back.

After a furtive glance up at the cliff Cathy stripped off her clothes, stuffed them into the bag, and stood wilting, and white in places, looking down at the water just below the level of the path. Then she crept down to where path and water joined and slid in.

The cold made her gasp, but she had been right, there was a stability in this water that there had not been before, and she warmed herself up with a rolling crawl that took her thirty yards out. She turned, and swam experimentally back for a few yards. Yes, it was manageable, although always underneath there was an ominous stirring, like the low growling of an animal that might become suddenly enraged. She turned out again towards Fiona, who still hung motionless in the water like a buoy.

Or rather, seemed to hang motionless. It was only when Cathy drew near that she realized that, every now and again, Fiona would ease away as if she were walking backwards, letting the gap between them narrow, but not quite close. The horrible doubt seized her that Fiona might be as capricious in her element as human beings were on land. Perhaps she had been wrong about that sublime innocence of hers. Perhaps there were traces of siren in her make-up. Perhaps she wanted revenge.

The water began to heave and plane, so that Cathy felt as if she were lying full length along a see-saw. She

138

lost her nerve. She floundered upright, treading water with the energy of a racing cyclist. "It's no good," she shouted. "I can't go on. I'm going back."

She turned back, and although shame welled up her fear was greater, and she began to claw her way back to the shore. The water was ill-mannered now, bucketing her about. She was moving as much from side to side as forward. She was growing tired. The cold was biting back now, and she had no reserves to fight it.

Cramp set in her left leg. Cathy forced herself to keep calm, turned on her back, and drew her leg up to massage the calf. This action made her sink under, and she swallowed water, and surfaced retching and coughing, and now she did panic, and began thrashing the water with her arms.

Fiona swam up to her side, took hold of her, and began propelling her towards the land.

No, there was no trace of siren in Fiona, nor of any other vagaries of the human make-up. She was suspicious of human blandishments. But she could not resist a cry for help.

She drew Cathy to the land. Once again Cathy found herself wrapped in the seaweed cloak, panting and shuddering, with the vile taste of brine in her nose and throat. But the cloak—not really seaweed, but of some material unknown—flushed her with warmth like old brandy in the stomach, and in no time she was sound again. She stood up, hanging on to Fiona, who was kneeling beside her on the path.

"Thank you, Fiona," she said.

She walked slowly up the path to where the bag was hidden. Even now she feared that Fiona might decide on safety and plunge back into the sea, but perhaps the seaweed cloak made her remain where she was. Cathy drew out her carrier bag.

Now: triumph or another disaster?

"You've given me a coat," she said. "Now I'll give you one."

And she pulled out the seal skin.

Fiona knelt there transfixed, like a child stunned by some present beyond its dreams. Slowly her face became suffused with joy, with gratitude, with adoration. She glowed in the gathering dusk. Her beauty was all but unbearable.

"*Mowes caradow,*" she said. "*Mowes cuf colon. Myrgh myr gerys. Myrgh ewngerys.*"

Cathy laughed and shook her head.

Fiona gathered all her powers for an effort.

"*Cowethes,*" she said. "*Friend.*"

"Good," said Cathy. "I'm glad we're agreed on that at last."

Fiona hugged her seal skin to her, stroking it, crooning over it. Cathy spoke to her like a district visitor.

"Now listen. I shall always come back. I shall always come back here. Every year. I shall wait for you. You must come to meet me. You must–"

But Fiona did not understand a word. Cathy drew the seaweed cloak more tightly about her shoulders.

"All right, I'll keep this cloak. I think it may have powers to fetch you back."

And then, as if speaking to a friend about a train, "And now I really think you should go."

She never saw Fiona's transformation. Somehow, in the few moments she spent in getting her own clothes out of the bag, the selkie had slipped away. And suddenly Cathy felt the anguish of parting.

"No, no–don't go–Don't go yet–"

But Fiona had disappeared. There was no splash, no ripple. Cathy strained her eyes seaward, but there was no sign of seal or girl.

She could do no more. Even now, of course, Fiona would not be perfectly happy. She must still retain a core of yearning for that kingdom under the water where they had all lived before the spell. But there could be no recovering that, any more than man could recover the Garden of Eden.

"Goodbye, Fiona," said Cathy.

Then she dressed and went home.

18

The elderly lady said what she had said every year at this time for many years.

"You can stay on if you wish, Fiona."

As always, the young girl smiled and shook her head.

As always, the elderly lady responded:

"No, very well. One day a year in this world is enough for you."

And so it was. In all her years of helping the suffering and downtrodden, both human and animal, and of campaigning against the trade in animals' skins in general, and the seal hunting trade in particular, and of trying to uphold sanity in a raging madhouse, and kindness in a jungle of cruelty, and of all else that went with her wide-flung organization, the Catherine Gascoyne Venture, she could not say that the world was much improved.

Of course, not everyone in it was bad. She counted among her friends the people of Cornwall, who admired her efforts to revive the old language. She had had a lot of help from her lifelong friend Lieutenant-Colonel Preston-Browne. It was said that many years ago he had made a habit of asking her to marry him, but at last he had accepted defeat and married a nice girl from Esher, seventeen years his junior.

Then there was Joe Stoneham, now retired from his

modest building and decorating business. He had been a tremendous help, and amazed everyone with his influence over her. It was even rumoured among her staff that she had had a long-standing affair with him, although the younger members found this incredible. But she had never married him, nor anyone else—fortunately for them all, said her staff, because Miss Gascoyne—although she was, of course, *fantastic*—would have driven any husband to his death in a few months. They said such things well out of earshot, because they were scared to death of Miss Gascoyne.

But in spite of such examples, she thought Fiona well-advised to return to the sea.

So, in the small hours of the morning, they left the cottage in Pendeen and drove to the little village of Polraddon. They did not drive through the village, but parked the car and walked along the Upper Cliff Road to the very edge of the cliffs.

They stared down at the moonlit beach. It was deserted. The area had never prospered. There had been a house on this cliff top once, but it had long since been pulled down.

"Well, my dear," said the lady.

The girl turned, took her in her arms, and hugged her as if she would never let her go.

"*Mowes caradow*," she murmured.

"*Mowes caradow*—'beloved girl'. I'm not such a girl now, Fiona. Sixty-eight next birthday."

Then: "There'll always be someone to meet you."

The girl undressed quickly. Cathy watched her go down the cliff path with the skin over her arm. Never since she had first given her that skin had she seen the actual change from human to animal, nor had she ever seen her enter the water.

She waited a while, then, brushing her hands

together as if to say "that's that", she began to walk back to her car.

"Now," she said to herself, "I must write to Clive and thank him for letting me use the cottage. And I must fix a lunch date with Joe."

She went on, not displeased with life, nor with herself. As she reached the crest of the hill she turned back and took a last long look at the sea, to where eternal youth was speeding away.